THE FIVE YEAR QUEEN

Janet Walkinshaw

By the same author

Long Road to Iona & Other Stories
Knox's Wife

THE FIVE YEAR QUEEN

Published in 2016 by FeedARead.com Publishing

A CIP catalogue record for this title is available from the British Library.

Cover design: www.hoggettcreative.co.uk
Cover photograph: Alex Whyte
Stewart & Tudor family trees: fuzzyblue

STEWART

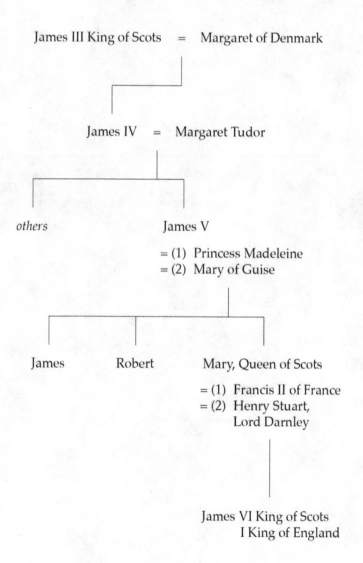

James III King of Scots = Margaret of Denmark

James IV = Margaret Tudor

others   James V

= (1) Princess Madeleine
= (2) Mary of Guise

James   Robert   Mary, Queen of Scots

= (1) Francis II of France
= (2) Henry Stuart,
           Lord Darnley

James VI King of Scots
        I King of England

TUDOR

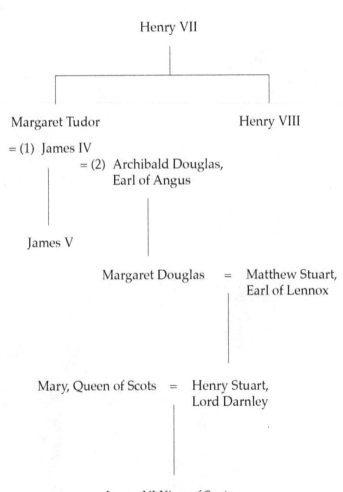

Henry VII

Margaret Tudor   Henry VIII

= (1) James IV

        = (2) Archibald Douglas,
                Earl of Angus

      James V

            Margaret Douglas   =   Matthew Stuart,
                                Earl of Lennox

Mary, Queen of Scots   =   Henry Stuart,
                          Lord Darnley

        James VI King of Scots
           I King of England

CHAPTER 1

It is a great joke. My sisters are not the only ones smiling behind their hands. The whole French court is laughing at the King of England: that he should offer for me. A big man wanting a big wife, they say. I say that a woman agreeing to be Henry's fourth wife would have to be foolishly ambitious or tired of living and I am neither.

People make haste to tell me that he only offers for me out of pique, for he knows I have already been offered to James of Scotland and Henry cannot bear that his nephew should have so easily what he cannot.

'The black is unfortunate,' says the painter. I do not reply. As a widow what else would I wear? I am impatient with the whole business. I do not see why I should have to co-operate in plans which will come to nothing. It is not M. Corneille's fault, for he is obliged to fulfil his commission to do a portrait of me whether he wants to or not. But as he considers, studying me from every angle, I see I need not have concerned myself with his feelings. He is thinking only of the task he has been given.

'Permit me,' he says and raises a hand to push my hood back to expose some of my hair. He nods, pleased, returns to his table and lifts a brush.

It is peaceful here, in this tower room which we only use when Chateaudun has too many visitors and there has been no such occasion since my husband died. The distracted servants have strewn fresh rushes on the floor but have overlooked the mouse droppings on the window sill. The only sound is the hiss of the midday rains. The shutters should be closed against the heat, but the painter needs the light. I am glad to sit, to obey his request to be still. It is a long time since I have had an hour to myself. There has been nothing but worry and agitation since the birth of my little Louis, named for his father who did not live to see him.

M. Corneille has undertaken to do the portrait in one sitting. It is to go to Scotland, along with the latest improved proposals for my dowry. King François is being generous, to demonstrate his love for his friend and ally the King of Scots. King James would prefer, it is said, another of France's princesses, but King François cannot reasonably be expected to part with a second daughter to the same man, having lost Madeleine to death so soon after her marriage. A non-royal bride merits a large dowry by way of recompense.

I have not agreed to this marriage and never will. I intend to stay here at Chateaudun, care for my sons, and mind the estate until they come of age. Then I will enter a nunnery, and become a Bride of Christ, as my grandmother has done. That is my destiny and they can negotiate how they like with portraits and dowries. I will not agree.

Meantime though, it is pleasant to sit and do nothing.

I met King James once but my memories of him are hazy. So much has happened to me since then. It is less than a year since I was one of the ladies attending the Princess Madeleine on their wedding day. At the

10

masque that followed the banquet King James sat beside his bride and laughed and applauded the romping lords and pages, who were using a mixture of French and Latin with here and there a sprinkling of Spanish and Italian, for the courts of Europe flocked to Paris for this wedding. When the collapsing sea monster had been dragged away and the laughing mermaids were helping the sailors pull off the brown wool of their beards, the floor was swept clear of soapy water and made ready for dancing.

I danced with my husband. King James partnered his new mother-in-law. As he moved down the set and I moved up, for a moment our hands touched as he turned me. For a moment I clasped my husband's hand and my other hand rested in the palm of King James. He did not look at me. His gaze was turned to the top dais where his bride crouched beside her father, her veil drawn half across her face to hide her fatigue, only her eyes showing. The more insensitive courtiers were already taking bets on how long the princess would survive the marriage. Some were even wondering whether she would survive the wedding night.

And now poor little Madeleine is dead and King François has offered me as a new bride to King James.

'Finished,' says the painter. 'You may look.'

It is small. It has to be, to fit into the pouch of a messenger. I could cover it with the palm of one hand. As I stretch forward to try this he tuts in warning, for the paint is still wet. He has ignored the whitewashed wall behind me and painted a green background. The red of my hair stands out in glowing contrast to the

11

black of my hood. He has painted the flesh of my neck and shoulders the colour of rich cream and has faintly delineated the chain that holds the crucifix, hidden in the bodice of my gown. He has painted me with a slight amused smile, almost coquettish. What have I to smile about?

'This is not a true portrait,' I protest.

'With respect, Duchesse, it is.'

THE CONVENT is as I remember it. As the Mother Superior welcomes me in, I discreetly sniff the air. There is the smell of the cheap tallow they insist on using for candles, and herbs, and underlying all, the faint odour of too many women occupying the same confined space.

The vesper-bell is ringing as I arrive and I make my way to the familiar chapel. I kneel at the back and try to pray, but I am too agitated to concentrate. Some of the nuns are casting sideways glances at me, but I pretend not to notice. Custody of the eyes is one of the disciplines taught as I was growing up here. I do not want to encourage any of these young women to break the rule, though I have forgotten it myself till now.

Mother is waiting for me as I follow the nuns out.

'Lady Philippa is ready for you.'

My grandmother is in the room set aside for meetings between the nuns and their visitors. Since I left the care of the convent I have not been allowed back into the private quarters, even though I am family. Here, our name means little. There are many worldly monasteries but this is not one of them.

My grandmother has not changed since I saw her last. Her face is a tapestry of fine lines in skin brown from years of working in the open air. She stands and moves with the lean vigour of a young woman, a vigour I can envy. I curtsey and she enfolds me in a warm embrace. She waits quietly till the storm of weeping passes, but as I pull myself together I see there are no answering tears in her eyes.

'The world has become too much for you,' she says.

'I would that I had never left here.'

'Nonsense. You were here for an education, not for a vocation. God did not want you for a Poor Clare. You were destined to take a place in the world with your husband.'

'But now my husband is dead.'

'You should thank God for two children. And many more to come.'

I struggle to speak. 'My baby son, my little Louis, died yesterday.'

She barely blinks. 'He has gone to be with Jesus. And with his father.'

Suddenly I am angry at this woman whom I have loved so long and so well. Does she no longer feel anything? The sight of my baby lying white and cold haunts me. I relive the frantic efforts we made to wake him and hear again the sobbing of the nursemaids. I swallow hard and try to still my hands in my lap.

'They are trying to force me into another marriage I do not want. Grandmother, if you told them not to do it to me, they would listen.'

'You must do as you are bid.'

'They cannot make me.'

13

'Would you disobey your mother and father? Would you disobey your king?'

'Grandmother, when God made you a widow, you were able to do as you wished. Why am I being denied a choice?'

'My dear, you are twenty-one years old. I was fifty-two when I came here. I did my duty all my life before that. I bore fourteen children. You have borne only two. You are not done yet.'

'I wish I had taken my vows and stayed. I would have been spared this pain.'

'The pain may be part of God's purpose for you. What you want is irrelevant.'

'What purpose could God have for me?'

'Perhaps it is His purpose that you go to Scotland.'

I feel the ground slipping away from me. I have been counting on the support of my grandmother. She was brought to Pont-au-Mousson in a litter, with pains in the head and limbs, her body swollen with dropsy. She told her anxious sons that she would stay for only two weeks of rest, but she never left. Life in the convent brought her back to health. She took the veil. She has now been here over twenty years. She sleeps on a straw pallet and wears the habit woven in the convent from coarse local wool. She daily thrusts her hands in the soil to plant vegetables, or into soap suds in the laundry. When I came here as a child to be educated I protested that only servants did such work and my grandmother chided me. It is all God's work, she said.

She is still speaking. 'Can you not trust God in His intent? This King of Scots who wishes to marry

14

you, they say he is a bulwark against the wicked heresies that are destroying Europe. It may be your task to aid him. Do not resist the call of God.'

I stay overnight, lying awake in a guest cell. All night I listen to the rustling of night creatures outside the window and hear the soft sounds round me, the muttered sleep of other guests, seeking solace here from their own troubles. I hear the bell ring to summon the nuns to matins, but I do not rise.

Is it God's purpose that I go to Scotland? Surely, surely, my grandmother is mistaken? The nuns see God's hand in everything, even the death of a child, even the wish of a king for a strong wife to breed sons.

I stay on for another day, praying, seeking guidance. After mass, when the priest has left and the women are once again alone, it is my grandmother's turn to address the community.

Lady Philippa speaks of the time when her son, my uncle the Cardinal of Lorraine, visited here. He was attended by many servants. He wore robes of the finest silk and his horse was caparisoned in crimson and gold cloth. The little girls in the convent who had never seen a prince of the Church before thought it was the king himself come to visit them.

He was visibly shaken by what he found. The Poor Clares live in poverty and simplicity. As the early fathers did, Lady Philippa reminds us now. As Jesus our Lord did himself. I did not understand, the cardinal kept saying. I did not understand. The community that night gave thanks that his eyes had been opened, that his conscience would cause him to examine his way of life.

The next day the cardinal sent his mother a fine bed like his own, with thick warm curtains and a soft mattress, with feather pillows and a silken quilt embroidered with peacocks. She slept on it for one night so as not to offend him and then had it removed from her cell.

Lady Philippa takes time to rub in the moral, that those who pursue their own ambitions can no longer hear God's voice, though the story reflects badly on the cardinal. As she finishes the story, she looks directly at me. I understand the message. But I have heard this story many times and have not failed to notice that each time my grandmother tells it she draws out a different moral, one suited to her audience and her purpose. Today she is telling me that I must do as I am bid, that I must not close my ears to what is demanded of me.

I have no illusions. I have heard often enough the talk of my father and uncles about war and peace to know that the safety of a country depends on friendships and treaties between kings. King James wants the protection of France. King François finds it useful to have an ally of Scotland, sitting as it does on England's northern flank, a reminder to that aggressive country that any war with France would have to be fought on two fronts. What other purpose is there? Where is God in all this? And where am I?

It is morning again. I leave early. In parting I kneel before my grandmother. She places her hands, twisted, blotchy, the nails broken and dirty, on my head and gives me her blessing.

'We will not meet again in this life,' she says. She reaches into the sleeve of her habit and pulls out

16

the Book of Hours which she has carried there as long as I can remember.

'I give you this. Read it every day. It will sustain you.'

I feel a surge of affection once more for this woman who was my comfort and mentor while I was growing up. But I tell myself as I ride away, I am a child no longer and my grandmother has been out of the world for too long.

'HUMOUR ME, my dear,' says the Abbot of Arbroath. 'I need tranquil company and pleasant conversation. I have been chasing all over France after the king and your father to finalise the details of the financial settlement and I am weary.'

'To no purpose.'

He reaches out and eases forward a rosebud whose stem has become twisted round its fellows. It will not straighten. He pulls from his pocket a small pair of gold scissors and snips it off. With a bow he presents it to me, my own rosebud from my own garden, with the air of a gallant. I tuck it into my bodice.

'I do not agree to this marriage.'

'I understand. But you know, so many negotiations come to nothing. I have been an ambassador in the service of King James long enough to understand that. Let's say it is a matter theoretical, like the talk of the alchemists, who would turn base metal into gold, but who never succeed, because base metal has its own qualities which it prefers to retain. It does not want to be gold.'

I cannot help it. I have to smile. 'I am base metal, Master Beaton?'

'Call me David.' He draws my arm under his. It is a familiarity no man has attempted since the death of my husband. I do not draw back. I was long enough at the court in Paris to sense when a man is making overtures and this man is not. He is as old as my father, but where my father is thin and battered from soldiering, David Beaton is smooth and rounded and his unfashionably short beard is blond and silky. His doublet is grey with sleeves of darker grey and a snowy white undershirt showing through the slashes, but somehow the effect is not restrained.

'We will be friends,' he says.

He speaks the clipped French of Paris. I have seen him at court, at a distance, but we have never before had any conversation. It is said he is the cleverest man to come out of Scotland.

'My father is not happy with this proposed marriage.'

'I know. He was good enough to speak plainly to me.'

'He is a plain man.'

My father wants the best for me. He would be anxious about these developments. Not like his brothers, my uncles. I can imagine them, particularly the cardinal, twittering with excitement at the thought of their niece as a queen. A queen of any country, it would not matter. If I were to marry into the Hottentots they would encourage it if it gave them more power.

David Beaton is still talking. 'Your father favours the offer from Henry of England. You would be closer and more able to return to France for a visit. You would certainly be richer. Henry is wealthy and is known to be most generous to his queens.'

'And then they die.'

'Perhaps he has merely been unfortunate.' But under his diplomatic words there is a chuckle and he is smiling, like everyone else when the matter of the King of England's search for a wife is mentioned.

I have had a letter from my mother, her usual spiky handwriting more unreadable than ever. My father is not well. His digestion is troubling him. The haste of this business is distressing. She has heard that the response of King François to the English proposal is that the contract with Scotland be drawn up as quickly as possible.

Looking now at the relaxed way David Beaton is murmuring his admiration of the roses sprawling over the wall, it is hard to imagine any agitation in the negotiations. My mother, who is totally in the confidence of my father, is particularly incensed that there has been a suggestion my estates from my first marriage should form my dowry. This is outrageous. These estates are my son's inheritance.

I say so now. 'I had understood, as did my father, that King François was to pay the dowry. It is he who is pressing for this match.'

'Of course the dowry should not come from your own estates,' agrees David Beaton. 'I cannot think where that idea came from.'

'You see the whole matter is impossible.'

'I have suggested that you yourself should be involved in the discussions of the financial arrangements. You must be totally satisfied before you commit yourself to this marriage.'

'I am not going to commit myself.'

'On the other hand, kings have to be obeyed, do they not? And it is the wish of your king that you marry into Scotland. It is not so very far away, you know. Travel is easy and King James has the finest ships in the world. I make the journey regularly myself. Many of your fellow countrymen are already settled there. I believe the head gardener at the Palace of Holyrood is a Frenchman. I am sure, now that I have seen your garden here, you would enjoy creating new gardens at King James's many palaces. The buildings are being modernised but the gardens are somewhat neglected. Our orchards, now, need new strains. I wonder if some from here would take. When I am at home I long for the pears and peaches of France.'

'I thought Scotland is all snowy wastes.'

He laughs. 'No, no, my dear. There are winter snows, but for the rest of the year the climate is pleasant. One becomes accustomed. But tell me why you do not wish to marry my king.'

I gather my thoughts once more.

'My son. He is not yet three years old. I will not leave him. That is one reason. Next, I am needed here to look after Chateaudun for him until he comes of age. This is my home. And I loved my husband. I do not wish another.'

Up until now whenever I have reiterated these reasons, everyone has come up with answers. My son would be well cared for by my mother. My youngest brother, who will be the last of Duchess Antoinette's children, for she has come to the end of her childbearing years, is almost the same age as my son, and there are all my other brothers and sisters and many cousins. He would go to live with them in the household at Bar-le-Duc, where I myself grew up. It is a happy place. His estates, and my own which I have from my husband, would be well looked after by my father and we have competent stewards.

A home is just the place where you live. I could make a home for myself in Scotland. There is no shortage of castles and palaces which I can decorate to my own tastes.

Love? Ah, love. Well, once I am married I will love my husband. Does not every woman?

But David Beaton says none of these things.

He paces by my side in silence. We pause at the end of the walk. From here we can look out over the houses of the village below and beyond them the river is already turning pink in the low autumn sun.

He says, 'I knew your husband. He was a fine man. I can understand that no other will equal him in your memory. I am glad yours was a love match. Every woman should have one such in her life. So should every man.'

What does he, a man of the Church, know of love matches? I do not say this, but he senses the question.

'I hope my Marion would be as faithful to my memory were I to die.'

'Your Marion?'

'I must not call her my wife. We were united when we were both young, before I was called to serve the Church and my country. We have eight children. I am sorry you will not know her. She never comes to

21

court. She is kept busy managing all the affairs of our little family.'

Two of my white doves flutter to the ground in front of us. Little François already has names for them, I tell Master Beaton. This one is Bibi and that is Sibo. He pulls some seedheads from the oregano plants and offers them, but the doves ignore him. They continue to peck at the ground and then fly away.

'I love France as I love Scotland,' he goes on. 'Your country and mine have long been friends and allies. We have aided each other against our natural enemies. The greatest of these enemies now is England. England would possess Scotland as she once possessed much of France. The greed of the English king is beyond measure. He wants it all, wealth, lands, power. Scotland and France must stand together. Your marriage would be one of the foundation stones of a new era of resistance against him.'

Darkness has fallen and as we turn I can see the windows of the house lighting up one by one as the servants bring candles and lamps. There is the gallery, the light travelling from window to window, there the dining hall, there the nursery, there my comptroller's room where he must still be working over the financial accounts. There is my private parlour where a fire will already be lit and to which I long to retreat, away from the burden of men's expectations.

'When King James was in Paris to marry the Princess Madeleine, he expressed his admiration for you then.'

'He hardly noticed me. He had eyes only for the Princess.'

'I assure you, he remembers you well. His desire for this marriage is not only a matter of diplomacy.'

'I just want to be left in peace.'

'What do your friends say? No doubt you talk about it to your friends. One friend perhaps? I know women have intimates they discuss everything with.'

I do not answer him. He is wrong. The decision has been a lonely one. I have not been able to talk to anyone about it, save my grandmother. It is not for want of friends, but this question is not like choosing the material for a new gown. Sometimes I have been on the verge of confiding in Marie de Pieris who is as close to me as a sister, but I hold back. I sense her watching me and waiting for me to speak, but I keep my own counsel. If she gives me advice which I follow and it turns out wrong, she would be the one to suffer most in her mind.

He changes the subject again. 'You know, in Scotland the dark does not fall suddenly as it does here. In summer it is light long into the night and darkness comes slowly even after the sun has set. Then the nightjars cry and the world settles itself slowly for rest. We call it the gloaming When the weather is fine, those are contented hours.'

He pats my hand where it still rests on his arm. We walk back to the house in silence.

When I reach my parlour I find I am still wearing the rosebud, bestowed on me as if it were a reward.

I pull out from my pocket my mother's letter and reread it. She ends with the thought that perhaps

God has great things in store for me in this world or the next.

But, I notice, Abbot Beaton did not bring God into it at all.

THE SMALL MAN stands with a knife in his hand. He bears the stains and I sense as I draw closer the stink of hard riding. He wears no livery. He is dressed in coarse brown wool hose and doublet, but I note that his jerkin and boots, though well-worn and splashed with mud, have the patina of the best leather well cared for. Two of my servants stand, one on either side, ready to jump on him if he makes a move.

'He claims to have a letter for you,' says M. de Curel.

M. de Curel would not normally interrupt me when I am going over the estate accounts with my comptroller of finance. These are not normal times. My whole household is unsettled. I cannot blame them. They all still grieve for my husband. They had my assurance that all would be as before, except that the estates would be under my control until my son came of age. That would not be much of a change, for my dear Louis left most of the day-to-day management to me anyway, but now this notion of a remarriage and exile has thrown everyone into a fever of uncertainty and insecurity. Visitors and messengers come and go and M. de Curel and the servants can only watch and wait.

'When we tried to search him he drew the dagger. He will not say who he comes from. My lady, he could be an assassin.'

'Who would want to kill me?'

The stranger pulls off his cap and bows. He is totally bald.

'You have a letter for me?'

'If you are the lady Duchess of Longueville.' He speaks the French of the Paris gutter, so I do not blame M. de Curel for his caution, but there is something in his accent that proclaims him a foreigner.

'I am.'

He is regarding me. 'Aye,' he says. 'You look like your picture.'

There has only been one portrait done of me.

'And who are you?'

He looks round at the men still standing, watchful, ready to protect me. One of them growls.

'Take care, my lady,' gasps M. de Curel. He is not accustomed to violence in my house.

'I'll give the dagger to the lady if she promises to give it back.' Without waiting for an answer he stretches the dagger out to me. My servants start forward but I stay them with a raised hand. Smiling now, he turns it so that the hilt is towards me. I reach out and take it. The blade is blackened. I have heard men talk of how cut-throats do this, so that the gleam of the steel will not betray their presence. I begin to feel hysterical laughter bubbling up inside me. After the events of the last few weeks it would not surprise me to find an assassin within the walls of my peaceful house. I swallow hard and am calm again.

I signal to the man to precede me. I follow him to a window embrasure where we can still be seen but not overheard. That he might have another weapon hidden about his person I am well aware. If he chooses to use it my men will kill him.

25

'Fergus MacLennan, at your service. I am the personal messenger of James Stewart, King of the Scots.' He pulls from under his jerkin a packet wrapped in waxed cloth. 'I am to wait for an answer.'

'Why the secrecy? May he not write to me?'

'There will be official letters. You will have had many of them.'

I nod.

'There are messages that are not official.'

I take the packet from him. 'Thank you, Monsieur Fergus MacLennan.'

He smiles back and looks me straight in the eye. 'When you speak my name like that it sounds like the lilt of the linnet in the spring.'

I am taken aback. It is one thing for Abbot David Beaton to speak to me in a familiar fashion, for he is the king's ambassador. If this mousy little man with the shiny pate is typical of the people in the employ of King James of Scotland, then his court must be very different from that of François.

I hand him back his dagger and signal to M. de Curel that all is well. He sends over a man to show M. MacLennan to the kitchen to be fed.

DID KING JAMES put it within its waxen protection himself, then handed it to the little brown man, or did he, as kings must do, dictate it to a clerk who dealt with it briskly as just another missive? There are several seals, which I examine carefully. None of them is the royal seal of the King of Scotland. David Beaton has shown me letters bearing the seal, so that I would know it. But I believe MacLennan when he says it comes from King James.

The last letter my dear Louis ever sent me lies in my desk in the box which was a gift from him on our wedding day. The box is of sandalwood inlaid in an intricate pattern of bellflowers and clover leaves in ebony and I keep only my most intimate documents in it. There were not many letters during our short marriage, though his duties at court often separated us, for my pregnancies kept me here at Chateaudun. Two pregnancies, one the sturdy boy I hear yelping with delight as he runs in the garden to escape his nursemaid, the other the baby now lying in the grave beside his father. My heart is still sore.

I know his last letter by heart. He had been taking medicine for a slight illness which his doctor said was a mild pox such as the country people had. He was recovering. He would be with me soon. But then the next day came word that he was dead. I still grieve for him, my beloved Louis, optimistic on that day of Pentecost in Péronne.

I do not want a love letter from another man.

I break the seals. King James writes a good strong hand, in French with only the occasional spelling lapse. I read it quickly through and then more slowly, surprised at what he has written. It is not a love letter. It is an appeal for help.

He is only twenty-seven years old, he writes, and has had a hard life, his father dying in war and leaving him, a two-year-old child, as ruler. He was brought up among men who used him as a pawn in their battle for power till he reached an age when he was able to assert himself, and for a long time he could not depend on the nobility of Scotland to be loyal to him. Now he rules a country which is peaceful and

27

growing in prosperity, but he is alone. On his border King Henry lurks, eager to seize Scotland, bribing and threatening in turn the nobles, who are easily swayed, and planting heretical ideas in the people.

All this alarms me, Madame, and I await your support and counsel.

My counsel? Can he truly believe that I can aid him? Can any woman? I reread the letter. He makes no promises to me. He is not offering me a comfortable life as his queen, that is not said. Instead he seeks a helpmeet whom he can trust, someone to rule by his side, someone to help him protect the Church, someone to help him defend his country against the King of England.

This is a letter from a king who loves his country. He is offering to put himself and that country into my care. As I read my heart is full of compassion. I think of my own boy, left fatherless at the age of two, my son whom I would have to leave behind. He too needs me, but he will be surrounded by a loving family and he is not destined to rule a kingdom. Can I ignore an appeal like this?

Is it pity I feel? Is pity enough for a marriage?

I sit for a long time with the letter in my hand. I have good reason for refusing to agree to this marriage. Nothing up till now has persuaded me that I should.

My grandmother told me God has a purpose for me. King François wants me to marry into Scotland. Could they, after all, see more clearly what I in my selfish blindness have refused to see? And so I feel, stirring within me, the desire to stand strong and firm beside this man who pleads for my aid. The Church is in danger. His country is in danger. Together we will protect both. I might not be able to give him my love, but I can give him my strength. I can help him build a country that will one day be as great as France.

I feel lightheaded. Suddenly I feel something shift inside me. It is almost physical. It is not happiness, that would be asking too much. It is relief. Relief that I can stop fighting.

There is a scuffle outside the door. It has grown dark and I have not eaten for many hours. No one has dared to come in to disturb me. I rise and ease the stiffness in my back and open the door to my women.

CHAPTER 2

Chateaudun is full of visiting Scotsmen, some with their wives, and great numbers of my Guise and Lorraine relatives.

My mother has taken responsibility for supervising the seamstresses and embroiderers and for weeks I have stood while they measure and stitch, slash and drape their materials round my body. She has ordered the finest lace from Bruxelles. King François has sent bales of cloth of gold and silver. The dressmakers' room is piled with brocade, heavy taffeta, plain and flowered velvets, silks and the almost transparent sarcenet. A dozen extra women have been brought in to make my wedding clothes and the gowns I will take to Scotland.

'You will look beautiful,' says David Beaton. He grows sleeker than ever. Soon he will be no longer just a mere commendator of an abbey in Scotland. King François has named him to the Holy Father as a Bishop of France and he is to be raised to the See of Mirepoix.

'Warm,' he says. 'You must have warm clothes.' King James has sent furs of lustrous Russian sable. These are being used to line a cloak and there is enough left to trim the sleeves of a winter gown. The English ambassador to Paris has travelled here with a bale of fine English woollen cloth and a miniature of King Henry, both gifts to show there are no hard feelings.

I am not surprised that Bishop-elect Beaton is taking an interest in my clothes. He is everywhere. There is no detail too trivial for his attention. His motto, I have learned, is *intentio, intentio.* It suits him well. He has spent hours with M. du Feu, my secretary, who is to come to Scotland with me as my comptroller of finance. We go over the details of the properties which are to be mine once I am wed to King James. The castles of Stirling, Threave, Dingwall, Doune, and the palace of Falkland, which Beaton assures me is indistinguishable from my beloved Chateaudun. Perhaps smaller, he concedes. There are earldoms which will be mine, Strathearn, Orkney, the lordship of Galloway, of the Isles. They are only names to me, but David Beaton knows all these territories. He can list the incomes which I will receive from each one. M. du Feu looks impressed as he notes the details. This wealth is beyond anything I have known.

When I am not being draped in cloth I am going over lists of people and interviewing those whom I would take to Scotland with me. M. de Curel is coming as Master of my Household. His daughter will be one of my ladies-in-waiting.

'How many?' I ask David Beaton, startled, when he lists the people I will need. 'Five ladies-in-waiting? Plus five maids-in-waiting? What will they do all day?' I recall my brief time as a lady-in-waiting at the French court, the tedium, the boredom of doing nothing.

'You will bring your own friends,' he says. 'But there are many Scottish families with daughters who expect to be honoured.'

There are the gentlewomen of my chamber, the cupbearers, esquires and ushers, the grooms, the muleteers, the stable boys, the cooks, the pâtissières, the people of the wine cellar and the pantry, the dressmakers, the launderers, the clerks. The tapissers have started gently and patiently packing the tapestries, while M. Columbell who has charge of the musicians is already fussing about how their instruments are to be protected from the sea air on the voyage. There seems to be no end to it and they will all have their own servants and all these people need to be housed and fed and clothed at my expense. I begin to think the income from my Scottish estates will not be sufficient.

'King James has a daughter, Jane, who will soon be of an age to be maid-in-waiting,' says David Beaton. A bastard daughter obviously, but he does not say so.

I ask 'How many children does the king have?'

'Nine acknowledged,' is the smooth answer.

'Are they about the court?'

'Not yet. They are all too young. They are destined for the Church and are being educated accordingly. John is to be prior of Coldingham and James primus will be Commendator of Melrose Abbey.'

'How old are they?'

'Nine and seven. The cleverest boy is James secundus. He will shortly be appointed prior of St Andrews. He is also nine years old. His grandfather is Lord Erskine, one of the king's closest advisers. Jane, of course, will be found a good marriage.'

As I listen to him making these plans for another man's children I wonder if little Jane will have any say in who she will wed. Perhaps a king's daughter, even bastard, will have her own way. But of course as one of my maidens she will be in my care. I can guide her future.

Some choices are easy.

'I would go with you even if you become too grand for me,' says Marie de Pieris.

'I will never be too grand. I would not want to leave you behind.' And indeed I could not imagine doing without her, for she makes me laugh when I would be serious. She has already thawed the reserve of the visiting Scotswomen who seem to sense the goodwill in her.

I choose my other ladies diplomatically, some my friends, some the daughters of our neighbouring families who expect to be honoured. M. de Curel can decide the servants who are to come.

My choice of chaplain is difficult. He must be congenial to me and to my ladies, for he will be by my side on many occasions. He must be of an age to be sensible. He must be learned, for I could not bear an ignorant man. He must be discreet, for as my confessor there will be no secrets from him and he will learn of matters which I would not wish the world to know.

The priest who has been in faithful attendance on the House of Longueville for many years and who passed into the service of my husband when we wed, declares himself too old to travel. He wishes to retire to a monastery. Looking at him, rheumy-eyed, walking with the aid of a stick, I cannot but agree with some relief. He sends a number of men to me but I cannot warm to any of them. One is conceited in his learning, another not learned enough. One has a sneer on his lips and I wonder if confessor to a woman, even a queen, is not a post he considers highly.

At last my mother recommends a priest known to her.

'He is the son of one of the tenants on our estate and has shown himself studious and quiet. Young, but devout. Would you consider him?'

I agree and soon Maître Jean Guillet is seated before me. He is indeed a grave young man, unsmiling, serious. He is thirty years old. He is tall and very thin, almost skeletal. As he bows to me I see that his tonsure is already spreading across his scalp and the thick black hair which surrounds it is flecked with white. I suspect he is nervous but he hides it well behind his still composure. Is this a man I can confide in? It is he who will have the responsibility to absolve me if I sin. I mentally correct myself. When I sin. It is not a burden to place lightly on the shoulders of a man so young.

I need someone older, more experienced. As I try to frame the words in my head that will not hurt him, I catch a glimpse of his hands, resting serenely in his lap. They are thin hands, with long fingers and short clean nails.

He catches me looking at them. He lifts one and thumps his chest in the universal gesture of contrition. *Mea culpa.* For the first time he gives me a rueful smile.

'It is my vanity,' he says. 'I grew up on a farm, as you know. We were all expected to work on the land. But when I turned more and more to books, it mattered to me that my hands were clean, that I did not soil the precious pages. I became obsessive about washing my hands. I was teased for it. Such fastidiousness is a cause for humour among children who will laugh at anyone they consider different.'

I know what he means. 'With me it was my height,' I say.

'The young do not see the elegance of the stately poplar in the common hedgerow.'

An unexpected compliment coming from a priest makes me smile, but it is not only that which makes me decide that Maître Guillet will come to Scotland with me as my personal chaplain. I feel comfortable with him. I think this man will be a gentle companion.

MY LITTLE SON is causing his nurse concern. 'François is fretting. We have tried to hide from him what is happening but he knows something is changing. So many people.' The girl is nearly in tears. 'Can you say to him you are only going away for a week and will soon be back? At that age they quickly forget.'

I do not want him to forget me and I cannot tell him lies. I lift him onto my lap and explain I am going on a long journey. He is to be a good boy and study his letters so that he can write to tell me everything he does. He gazes at me round-eyed and troubled. I struggle to hide my own emotion, for I know he will grow up without me. I press my arms round him, but this is embarrassing to a little boy trying to be a man and the tears quickly dry up as he wriggles out of my arms.

Later I see him in the garden being cooed over by the visiting Scotswomen. They are applauding him as he marches up and down waving a wooden sword and boasting of his soldier grandfather.

KING JAMES has not come to France himself for our marriage ceremony, but has sent Lord Maxwell to act as proxy. I am disappointed at the king's absence, but only mildly. Since he was in France last year for his first wedding, perhaps he cannot afford to come again. Besides, this will delay the consummation of our marriage and I am not sorry for that.

The daytime entertainment for the Scotswomen has been difficult. The men are happy. They ride out daily with my father and my uncles. My father would have liked to provide jousting tournaments but the men have not brought their gear and there is little time to organise it. There are numerous displays of swordsmanship and hours spent at the butts in competition, French against Scots.

Conversation with the women is stilted, for they have poor French and I, as yet, have little of the Scots tongue. We can only smile at one another as I show them over the house, while they politely admire our tapestries and the paintings hanging in the gallery. I depend on Marie. She has the talent, which I have not, of making instant friendships and she chatters away to the women, who are cautiously warming to her.

The evenings spent in banqueting and music are long and tiring. When the tables are cleared from the hall the visiting Scots fiddlers strike up and the room reverberates to the thumping beat of their dancing, wild and fast, dances which are more like the dances of the peasants and not like the courtly dances we are used to. Only the men dance. The noisiest of them is Lord Maxwell. The floor shakes and my head aches. With a final screech from the men the dance ends and Lord Maxwell returns to his seat beside me. He slaps his thigh as he sits down.

'Vigour in the dance, valour in war.' His speech is slurred.

He sits too close to me and I feel the heat of him. His knee nudges mine. He takes my hand in his and pats it. 'You're a bonny lass,' he says. 'By God, I wish I were Jamie's proxy in more than the flummeries in the chapel.' Before I can respond he pales and rises to his feet and lurches off, most likely to vomit.

David Beaton slides into his place. The Scots fiddlers are resting now. My own musicians have begun to play some slower airs and everyone is watching the dancers.

'My Lord Maxwell is one of the king's most valued advisers,' says Beaton. 'A brave soldier.'

'Indeed.'

'He supported the king in his struggle for power. His son was brought up in the royal household. Maxwell is so trusted that he governed Scotland as regent while James came to Paris to marry the Princess Madeleine.'

'I understand.' I do. I must tolerate the man. He is a friend of the king.

'That said,' says David Beaton softly, 'the man is a boor.' And he has gone before I can judge whether I have heard him rightly.

I am relieved to escape to my room with Marie. I am feeling weepy and tired, tired of being surrounded constantly by people, tired of being the centre of attention. Thankfully, we throw off our heavy gowns and dismiss the maids. It is a relief to flop onto cushions. Marie is the only person I can truly relax with. Even my mother frowns at me if she sees me drooping.

We practise a few words in the Scots language. 'Tak tent,' I say, and she giggles. Take care.

'The Lord Seton,' I continue. 'Seeks you out often, I think. You can hardly turn round without bumping into him.'

Lord George Seton is lively and quick. He is of slender build, and I would judge he has not the weight to make his mark in jousting but his swordsmanship is second to none, and he has the steady eye and hand of a skilled archer. I am not the only one to have noticed his partiality for Marie. He seems content to sit with the ladies in the evening and sing in a lilting light tenor to the accompaniment of his lute. He seems unaware of the meaningful glances the Scotswomen send to one another.

We know little of the circumstances of the man. Marie is to come to Scotland with me. I do not want her to be hurt.

'He is one of King James's closest friends. They grew up together,' she says.

'In his growing up the king sired nine bastard children. How many does Seton have?'

She scrambles to her feet. 'He is honourable. He is a widower. Why should he not seek my company?'

I try to soothe her but she is angry with me, and that alone tells me that matters with Seton have progressed further than might be sensible.

'You will be my responsibility in Scotland.'

39

'I am nobody's responsibility save my own.'

'I will be answerable to your parents if ill befalls you.'

'Nothing ill will happen.'

She is in tears. I put my arm round her and give her a hug. 'There now,' I say. 'We quarrel for nothing.'

'I hope you will not become too serious, when you are a queen.'

'I will not,' I say. 'Not with you there. But you must still be careful. When away from home men act in ways they would not normally dare to. In ways they may hope will be forgotten when they are among their own people again.'

THE MARRIAGE CEREMONY passes in a dream. From Lord Maxwell by my side I catch a gust of stale breath and I see the sweat standing out on his forehead. Prompted by my uncle the Cardinal of Lorraine he makes the correct responses. He puts the diamond ring on my finger and I am married.

I do not spend the night alone, this wedding night that is not a true wedding night. I invite my little sister Louise to share my bed, knowing she is thrilled to be chosen. I keep her awake, not difficult since she is almost feverish with excitement. But exhaustion overtakes her and she sleeps and I, desperate to keep the ghosts at bay, concentrate on King James, my new husband, but he is hazy. I can barely remember what he looks like. I wonder if he, too, is lying awake thinking of me, or whether the day for him has been like any other.

But as I drift off to sleep the arms I sense embracing me are those of my dear Louis and I cry his name aloud. My sister stirs in her sleep. I force myself to lie still and give myself up to the ache in body and soul.

THE SCOTTISH GALLEONS are moored along the quayside at Le Havre. The maze of masts and ropes stretches up and up and up to the sky like a man's crazy attempt at embroidery and as I watch the sailors clambering over the rigging I feel dizzy and have to hold on to Marie to stop myself falling.

Le Havre is large and all is activity. Heavily laden merchant vessels under foreign flags are tacking out of the bay and others rest at anchor waiting to enter. King François has offered his warship *Riall* to protect us on the journey and she is anchored beyond the entrance to the harbour. Those of my friends who are not to remain in Scotland will return on her. On the beach the French galleys which are to escort us are already drawn up, the rowers, prisoners of war I am told, settling down round them with food and flagons of wine, some throwing dice, some sleeping. We are to sail on the next tide.

M. de Curel stands with a list of the people as they file aboard. His two assistants are checking off on their lists the final loading of chests containing linen, plate, books, tapestries and I do not know what else. Most has already gone aboard, for the men have been working by torchlight all night. My horses are loaded onto the *Morisot*. I stroke the nose of Mouflon and murmur words of reassurance to her while she is blindfolded to be led up the plank. The groom assures me she will be well cared for. Horses, he tells me, travel all the time on ships.

41

I am to travel on King James's personal flagship, the *Mary Willoughby*. It is the biggest and finest of the vessels. Four masts and a high many-storeyed stern stretch above us. That is where our cabins will be. Banners, one bearing the royal arms of Scotland, another my own arms, hang limply by a rope, waiting to be hoisted as soon as I set foot on board.

I become aware of raised voices further along the quay.

'My lords, what is the matter?'

It is David Beaton who explains. 'It seems I am not to travel with you in the *Mary Willoughby*, Your Grace.'

'You will travel in the *Salamander*,' says Lord Maxwell. He is the calmer of the two.

'Who decides this?' I ask.

'I do. As Lord Admiral I decide the disposition of the king's ships.'

Round about us men scurry about their duties, keeping their faces turned away.

'It is my place to be with the queen.'

'You will travel on the *Salamander* or you will remain in France. Which no doubt you would prefer to do.'

David Beaton looks at him, breathing heavily.

'My Lord Maxwell,' I say, trying to keep my voice light and friendly. 'Could you allow this, to please me? I would value the bishop's company on the journey.'

'Abbot Beaton has been allocated a cabin on the *Salamander*. The arrangements cannot be changed.'

He makes a cursory bow to me and strides off, snapping his fingers at two sailors who are adjusting a gangplank on the *Morisot* as the rising tide lifts her.

'Lord Maxwell mislikes my company even for a day, far less for a week of a voyage,' says Beaton.

'It will not matter,' I say gently. 'But why do you dislike one another so much?'

'No particular deed or word. But he's a Lutheran and he only lightly disguises it.'

'A Lutheran?' I feel a chill. 'There are Lutherans in Scotland?'

'Not for long,' says Beaton. 'They will be rooted out and destroyed.' He glares after Lord Maxwell, who is now talking to the ships' captains grouped round him, no doubt giving final orders. 'Be they ever so powerful.'

'Does King James know? That there are Lutherans. That Lord Maxwell is one.'

'James knows everything.'

The Lutherans preach heresy. Nurses have been threatening children these twenty years with the name of Martin Luther. He has been the cause of all the misery that has overwhelmed the nations. It is his followers who caused the King of England to break with Rome and split Christendom. They are wicked, wicked people.

King James sent a Lutheran as his proxy at my wedding. I cannot believe it. I grasp the crucifix round my neck and send a silent prayer to St Clare that David Beaton in his contempt for Maxwell has been mistaken in what he has told me.

We set sail and I give myself up to the new experience. My father and Louise are travelling with

43

me. They are to stay in Scotland for a few weeks to see me settled. Louise is sick, along with many of the other women, and my physician and the maids are kept busy ministering to them as they lie on their bunks in agonies. I hover for a short time trying to help but I am clearly not wanted.

'Never again,' gasps Marie. 'Holy Mother of Jesus, let this be over and never again will I set foot on a ship.'

I have no such problems. I have my sea legs, as Captain Wood calls it. Captain Wood is lean and brown. When he bows to me I think his thick eyebrows are full of salt but it is only grey. 'It is good,' he says. 'King James is a great sailor. It may please him to take you on his travels if you can stand the motion.'

We sail east, through La Manche. I watch the coast of France drop away behind us with sadness. I do not know when I will see my homeland again, if ever. Soon the Low Countries lie to the south of us and we turn north into the open sea. The sea roads here are busy with shipping. There are the flags of many nations and I pick out the Scottish flag prominent among them.

The sea is calm and the wind steady. On the third day the invalids begin to recover and make their way onto the deck. On the third day too the French galleys signal their farewells and turn back towards home. Occasionally a small, fast ship approaches from up ahead, makes a signal to the *Mary Willoughby* and veers off, to race away again.

'What ship is that?'

'A scout. King James has ordered her to travel ahead of us to check the English coastline for danger.'

'Why should there be danger?'

'The English king is mad,' says Lord Maxwell. 'And there is no knowing what madmen may do. Maybe he would think to kidnap you.'

Perhaps the tension in him arises from the great responsibility he has been given. I resolve that tonight at dinner I will find the words to show I appreciate the care he is taking of me and mine.

He and my father pace the deck every day, their heads together. Such conversation as I overhear is concerned with military matters. Both are soldiers, but while my father has fought almost to the death for France in war, Lord Maxwell has only fought when he is defending Scotland and then only against the English and their mercenaries. My father successfully hides his contempt for such small-scale activity.

But they unite in a dislike of the English soldiers.

'Barbarians, the English,' sneers Lord Maxwell. My father agrees. They can succeed in short sharp battles, but win or lose they murder, rape and plunder among the people, destroying crops and dwellings in an orgy of destruction. The English king prides himself on being a true Christian knight, but he leads a barbarous nation. They walk on, in agreement. It is rare for my father to be free of responsibility and he is relishing the leisure.

I am content to sit on the deck in the sunshine and watch the rise and fall of the water, the changing blues and greens and the dolphins that leap alongside the vessel. The regular creaking of the masts and ropes is soothing, with only now and again the hard crack of the wind in a sail as the helmsman eases the ship round to catch every breath of air. We are not racing against time, says Captain Wood, better a comfortable journey than a fast one.

From time to time Captain Wood is able to sit with me, though all the time he is watching and listening to every movement of the vessel. He has been sailing since he was old enough to walk, first on the fishing boats and then on merchant ships and the king's warships. Now he is one of the king's captains and proud of it. There is not a stretch of coastline from the icy north to the coast of Africa that he does not know. His voice has a light, singing lilt and he speaks French with an intermingling of words from other languages.

'I have sailed the *Mary Willoughby* for many years,' he tells me. 'She is the king's favourite. She was captured from the English. King Henry sent ships to intercept Scottish merchants, but the men of the Western Isles are the finest sailors in the world.'

Such braggadocio, I think as I listen to his soft voice, and wonder if all Scotsmen are the same, but I chide myself for lack of charity, for what do I know of the sea or ships and perhaps he speaks the truth.

'King James has had her strengthened and refitted. She has done this voyage between Scotland and France many times.'

My cabin is very well appointed with everything I need. It is big enough for my own bed to be set up and I am as comfortable as I would be at home.

I must learn to stop thinking of Chateaudun as home. My home will be Scotland.

From time to time as we tack westwards the English coast appears. On sleepless nights when I come up on deck for air I can see the occasional flare of a beacon on the land.

'They are monitoring our progress,' says the captain. 'All Europe knows you are making this journey.'

'I am not that important,' I cry.

He says nothing. I shiver, though the night is warm.

Maître Guillet seems to thrive, his cheeks glowing and his eyes sparkling as he paces the deck. oblivious to the occasional scowl from a mariner, for there are many superstitions about priests on board ship. He stands in the bow of the ship, throws back his hood and lets the spray wash over his face. Sometimes he stands at the stern shouting into the wind psalms exalting God.

'The sea does strange things to men,' says the captain.

The days drift into one another. Sometimes the *Morisot* sails closer. I wave to David Beaton on her deck and he inclines his head in return. I have not spoken to him since the argument on the quayside. I hope he is not angry with me but it was not my fault. How could I overrule Lord Maxwell?

'George,' I ask Lord Seton. 'Does David Beaton fly into a rage often?' It is evening and we are in the privacy of the saloon with only a few of my ladies. He is picking out an air on the lute.

'He was already . . . ' Seton stops.

'Already?'

'Tired. The anxieties of the preceding weeks.'

Later, I ask Marie if Lord Seton is aware of some matter I should know about.

'It's likely nothing. Master Beaton was unhappy because of the arrangements for the wedding.'

'But he organised it.'

'Not the ceremony. He was not part of the planning for that. He was angry because he was not allowed to be one of the clergy officiating at the wedding and the mass.'

They were all members of my family, the cardinal and bishops at my wedding. But I should have given it some thought instead of leaving it to others. I should have asked that Beaton be included. It had not occurred to me.

WHEN IT SEEMS this dream-like interlude will go on for ever, Lord Maxwell says 'That is Scotland.'

We have passed Berwick which, he tells me, marks the border with England. We sail on past low-lying land and a great estuary, then we round a headland into another estuary where people crowd the beaches to watch us sailing past.

As the *Mary Willoughby* turns in towards the land the *Morisot* and the *Salamander* veer off and continue north, and are soon out of sight.

'They are not landing with us?' I ask Lord Maxwell.

'They have gone on to St Andrews.'

'We are not going there?'

'Not yet. We were sighted some time ago and word will already have been sent to the king there. The arrangement is that you will spend the night at the Castle of Balcomie, which is nearby and has been made

48

ready for you. They are preparing a welcome in St Andrews. There has to be a formal entry. It would not be fitting for the Queen of Scots to land at the quayside like any common traveller.'

We round into a great bay and there, pulling out from the land, are a mass of small boats laden with people. Louise is clinging to me and she is crying for no reason that I can fathom, while Marie hangs over the railings and waves madly back at the people in the small boats.

My ladies and I hastily change out of our clothes, salt-spray stained, into clean gowns.

The captain comes forward.

'Thank you for a good journey,' I say. 'Shall we meet again?'

'Aye, we will that. This ship is one King James often travels on.'

The ship's tender is lowered and manoeuvred alongside and we are helped down into it. The seamen row to a small harbour and I stand in the boat while it is tied up alongside. I take Lord Maxwell's hand to step onto Scottish soil. In my mind I have been rehearsing this moment for weeks. There is a cheer from the crowd.

'My lord, what date is today?'

'The twelfth of June. It wants but two weeks to midsummer.'

'Trinity Sunday,' says Maître Guillet at my side.

'I will remember this day.' I speak loudly so that all may hear, assuming a few in the crowd will speak French and translate for the others.

A man steps forward and bows. The woman hovering by his side curtseys and as she bobs up again her gaze flickers over me from my hood to the hem of my gown and back again, taking in every detail. I must accustom myself to being stared at.

Her husband makes a speech of welcome. Thankfully George Seton has now disembarked and translates for me. 'Your Grace, this is Sir John Learmonth. He welcomes you to Scotland to his home. He will try to make you and your household as comfortable as can be while you are here.'

I reply as best I can in the little Scots I have, reflecting ruefully that even though I have been studying the language for weeks, the first time a man speaks to me I do not understand a word.

I take a few steps forward and nearly fall, for the earth seems to sway under my feet. Behind me more than one of my ladies is weeping with relief to be on dry land.

There is a cool wind despite the season. The air smells differently from the breezes round Chateaudun, less fragrant. The light wind sighs through the long grass on the hill. After the days at sea everything seems bright, the green grass on the hill, the white sand crowded with the watching people.

Balcomie Castle is no more than a modest tower house. The small chapel is tucked away in a corner of the courtyard and here I kneel with as many of my household as can squeeze in, while Maître Guillet leads us in giving thanks to God for a safe journey. My own prayers are focused once more on an avowal that I will do my best with the task I have been given.

As we emerge from the chapel, blinking in the sunlight, a stranger is dismounting from his horse. For a moment I think it is King James, my husband, come to welcome me, but then I see it is not.

The newcomer sweeps off his feathered cap and bows low, an elaborate courtly bow. He is dressed in a scarlet and green doublet and the sleeves of his shirt are slashed to reveal puffs of red silk. He stands out in sharp contrast to my people in their dark travelling clothes.

'Dear God, the king has sent his papingo,' mutters Lord Maxwell behind me.

And I, whether from the heightened emotion or from weariness, or because he does indeed look like a flamboyant parrot in the midst of a crowd of rooks, I laugh aloud. Immediately I realise I have made a mistake. It takes the newcomer only an instant as he straightens up to clear the flash of offence from his face, but I see it. I am silenced.

'Oliver Sinclair of Pitcairn at your service, Your Grace,' he says in smooth French. 'His Grace the King has sent me to ensure you are comfortable. He thought it best that you rest after your journey. All is prepared for your formal entry into St Andrews.'

He bows again and stands aside to allow me to follow Sir John to my first meal and my first night in Scotland.

BY TEN O'CLOCK the next morning I am ready to meet my husband. I have changed into a gown of cream brocade trimmed with red velvet. Today there is to be my formal entry into St Andrews and I have to look like a queen. This gown occasioned much thought and planning at Chateaudun. The royal colours of Scotland are yellow and red but yellow does not suit

51

my complexion. Cream is a compromise and one I hope will be appreciated.

Standing beside me at the highest window in the castle, Sir John Learmonth points north to where the dust of the cavalcade can be seen. Soon it is in sight, a long line of horses carrying riders in bright colours, heralds bearing flying pennants and liveried outriders in scarlet and yellow. The procession is led by the king's standard bearer, flying the lion of Scotland.

By the time King James enters the courtyard I am waiting on the step, with my ladies around me. He dismounts and bows formally then comes forward, seizes both my hands in his and kisses them. There are delighted murmur around us.

'This is a happy day.'

His French is heavily accented but clear enough to me, for he speaks slowly.

Long nose, long chin hardly hidden by his beard. I remember that. I had forgotten the tawny hair, not unlike my own, now bright in the sunshine as he turns to wave his cap at the people crowding the courtyard. The sunlight catches on his cheeks the old scars of smallpox, though faint enough not to be disfiguring. Not, I realise with a sinking heart, as tall as me. I try to slump into my spine slightly to compensate. Thankfully my shoes and boots have been flat ever since I grew tall in adolescence.

I feel shy and cannot think what to say to my new husband. He asks if I have had a pleasant journey,and I assure him it was most comfortable. The ship is very fine. He looks pleased at this. I become conscious of the stares of the courtiers now dismounting and crowding in behind the King. Oliver Sinclair has moved to stand at the king's right shoulder.

The king greets my father, whom he remembers from his visit to the French court over a year ago to wed Princess Madeleine. Graciously he refers to that occasion now.

'But sorrow has turned to happiness with the arrival of your beautiful daughter,' he says. 'And another.' He turns to my sister Louise who blushes as she curtseys, overcome with bashfulness.

There comes a diversion. He has a surprise for me, he says. He signals and my horse, Mouflon, offloaded from the *Morisot* at St Andrews the night before, is brought forward. Mouflon is wearing a fine new saddle of Spanish leather, intricately decorated in red and black. It is James's welcoming present to me. The cloth under the saddle is woven with the symbols of our two countries, the thistle of Scotland and the lily of France.

'It is the custom here for a new bride to ride pillion behind her husband,' says James. 'But I thought as you have a reputation for being a fine horsewoman and need no protection, you would prefer to ride your own horse.' I am not sure if I deserve the compliment, but he is right. Riding pillion is acceptable for shy young virgins who need to hide their blushes in their new husband's back. For a widow like myself it would be ridiculous.

I am overcome with his forethought and my thanks to him are genuine and emotional. He shifts slightly as if embarrassed, while I stroke the muzzle of the horse. My groom, who has been leading her, winks at me. 'None the worse for the journey,' he murmurs.

James moves closer and for a moment I think he is going to lift me up into the saddle. But I am too big, I nearly protest in panic and then realise in time I have misunderstood. He only wishes to take my hand to lead me into the castle where Lady Learmonth is waiting with a table spread with food and wine.

At last we take our leave of Sir John and his wife. The king and I mount our horses and set ourselves at the head of the procession. My ladies wrap a cloak round me to protect my gown from the dust of the road and we set off. Behind us come my father and Louise, followed by the two households. The courtiers sort themselves out, French and Scottish riding side by side, men and women, two by two.

The land is pleasant and stretches away in gentle hills. The rigs are growing well with oats and barley. We make slow progress on the road, for at every cluster of dwellings we must stop while James speaks to the people. Women hold up their little ones to see us pass.

When I was serving as a lady-in-waiting to the daughters of King François I occasionally took part in royal entries, but always I have been well back, almost anonymous, surrounded by other ladies, escorted by courtiers. Now I learn what it is like to be at the front and to be the focus of everyone's interest.

The roadside is becoming crowded. St Andrews comes into view, a town of soaring pinnacles and towers and towering above all, the great cathedral. James reaches over and takes my hand. 'Courage,' he says. 'They will love you.'

We approach the town along the river, circling the wall. As we halt at the gateway the gates slowly open and from the high arch a painted cloud is lowered. It splits apart into two halves to reveal a child dressed as an angel who recites a speech of welcome in a high, shaky voice. Again, as with Sir John the day before, I cannot follow the words. It is fortunate that after we dined last night, Oliver Sinclair gave me a paper with the words of the welcome written on it in both Scots and French so that I could understand it. There was also the appropriate reply which I must make.

'That is thoughtful,' I said.

He shrugged as if indifferent. 'It is Lyndsay's doing,' he says. 'He organises these things.'

I press him for more information and learn that Sir David Lyndsay's official post is as Snowden Herald, but since the Lord Lyon is an old man in poor health, Sir David includes in his duties not only the organisation of the court's entertainment but also all of the ceremonial. He was not in the King's train so I have not yet met him. At the French court the poets and players who can organise masques and entertainments are highly prized. As I took the paper from Oliver Sinclair I noted the sneer on his face. He clearly does not value Sir David Lyndsay or his talent.

Now I am being told that all the hearts of Scotland are open to me and that I have to love God, obey my husband and keep my body clean, according to God's commandments.

The child – I am not totally clear whether it is a boy or a girl, for the long white shift and white silver-spangled wig are unsexing – leans precariously

55

forward on the cloud and presses a large shiny wooden key into my hand.

'The key to the Kingdom of Scotland,' murmurs James.

I am able to make the pretty speech in return. I hope they do not hear the nervousness, equal to that, I suspect, of the little angel. Then we ride through the gates and into the town, to a deafening roar from the crowd and a carillon of bells from all the churches.

We ride up the hill and enter a broad street lined with solid stone houses, all draped with bright banners and at every window people are leaning out to see us. At every station along the route there is a new pageant or a tableau, more speeches, more music, but now I only have to nod and smile. The richness of all that is shown to me is impressive and, lacking language and knowing the words would not be heard anyway over the music and noise of the crowd, I clap my hands together to show my delight. It appears that every guild in the town, the jewellers, the goldsmiths, the tailors, the cobblers, the masons, the bakers and everyone else has insisted on having a part.

Alertness is needed, I realise. I have never understood before how tiring it is to be at the head of a procession. In the past, well back, the poetic speeches and plays were over and the tableaux beginning to droop and scatter by the time I and the other ladies reached them. Now I have to see everything without once relaxing my attention. The first impression I make may colour my life here. My face begins to ache.

Now at last we are at the gates of the towering cathedral where the formal welcoming party waits. The assembled burgesses are in their robes with their chains of office. There are arrayed the churchmen, seemingly hundreds of them, for this is the ecclesiastical capital of Scotland. The bright canonical robes are all the more splendid beside the groups of monks in white and grey and black. The Archbishop of St Andrews comes forward to welcome me and behind him among the crowd of clerics I see Bishop David Beaton smiling at me and I nod to him, pleased to see a friend.

We dismount and the king leads me through the cathedral, packed with people, to the high altar where we kneel and give thanks. Then we are seated and the archbishop begins the mass.

I badly need to pass water but no one seems to have thought of pausing or making provision for this. I lay on my lap the large wooden key which I have been clutching all this time and stretch my fingers. The silver has peeled off onto my sweating hand.

I control my bodily weakness. I close my eyes and allow the dear familiar Latin liturgy to flow over me.

WITH ONLY ONE more night's rest I must be married in earnest. This is the formal confirmation of our marriage, but to me it is a truer wedding day than the proxy ceremony in France.

I am wearing the same gown I wore then, cloth of silver with a hood sewn with diamonds. By my side James is almost as magnificent for he too wears cloth of silver, trimmed with white velvet. He looks serious, intent on the words of the archbishop. We sit together facing the congregation while the nuptial mass is being sung and I become conscious once more of all eyes on me. This is what it will always be like, always watched, always on display. Do not droop. These were my mother's words to me as I was growing, conscious of my height. Do not droop. I wish she could be here.

Above the singing of the choir can be heard the exuberance of the crowds outside, waiting for our exit from the cathedral to signal the start of the feasting and games which have been set up for them. Today is their day. Tomorrow will begin the grand tournament of knights so that the all the lords and their squires may show off their skill.

THERE HAS BEEN little mention of the other queen in Scotland, the Dowager, who was the Princess Margaret Tudor. She rarely comes to court now, living quietly at her home near Perth.

When I say to James I would like to know her his answer is abrupt. 'You will have little to do with her.'

I persist. 'She is your mother.' He repeats, 'You will have little to do with her.'

Later, of course, I learn the story.

When Margaret Tudor came north to marry the king, James's father, she was a child on the verge of womanhood, beautiful and gracious as befitted an English princess. She brought with her a Treaty of Perpetual Peace. In due course several children were born. The old King of England died and Queen Margaret's brother Henry became king. Young and hot-headed, Henry declared war on France. In honour of the older alliance between Scotland and France, the Scottish king in turn had to make war on England. He marched at the head of his army, the fairest and best of the men of Scotland. The armies met at Flodden Field and the King of Scots died.

Her son, the new King of Scots was less than two years old. Queen Margaret had the regency, for that is the tradition here. All might have been well but she married again in haste that offended everyone and so she lost the regency. Her new husband, Archibald Douglas, Earl of Angus, was a man greedy for power and kept the young King almost a prisoner.

Later she divorced Angus and married Lord Ruthven and now she wishes to divorce him too. Do they then so lightly take their marriage vows, these Tudors?

Perhaps, free once more, she would return to Angus, and my husband, for whom Angus is his bitterest enemy, refuses to allow his mother to divorce.

KING JAMES PRESIDES over a table of men at the evening banquet. Despite the ill-feeling between them the Dowager Queen Margaret must be given her place on this day of all days, the day of her son's marriage.

She has the place of honour among the women on my side of the hall. Beside the other ladies she looks drab, in a gown cut in the style of several years ago, with yellowing lace trimming the yoke which frames her fleshy shoulders and chins. I have difficulty imagining what she must have been like as a young princess.

'You look sturdy,' she says. 'Kept your figure. Courses regular? Two children so far, that right? I had six. Only James survived infancy. Let's hope you can do better.' Her French is rapid but ungrammatical and with such a heavy accent I have to concentrate to follow her. She has paused for breath and I gather myself together to respond.

'I hope so.'

'All a bit bewildering I expect. I went through it too, near forty years ago now. Soon settles down. Let's hope you have more good fortune than I had. Watch out for Arran.'

She lifts her knife and gestures towards a woman seated well above the salt. 'That's Arran's wife. Until you have a son Arran is the heir.' The Countess of Arran, aware she is being spoken about, for how can she not know with the Dowager scowling at her, is watching me as a child will watch a beetle climb a leafstalk, waiting for it to fall. From time to time she exchanges words in a whisper with her neighbours, who all turn to look at me.

'Better you anyway than Erskine's daughter.'

A servant holds a cloth up to hide Queen Margaret while she spits out some gristle. She signals for more wine.

'What was I saying?'

'Lord Erskine's daughter.'

'She's not here. Nothing against Erskine. That's him, four down from your father, the one in grey. He had the care of Jamie when he was a boy but I'm not blaming him. That was a nonsense, Jamie thinking he could marry her, as if her husband would give her up just like that. It was as well David Beaton put his foot down. Refused to ask the Pope for his consent so that was that. For James to marry the girl would have set all the court at one another's heads. He had to marry into France. All knew that. It was the treaty. You look a good choice.'

60

I bow at the compliment, and she talks on. I cease to attempt to follow all the names she throws at me. No one has told me before that the king wished to marry another woman, one of his own people, although it might cause trouble. When was this? Before or after Madeleine? Does David Beaton then have such power that he can dictate to the king whom he cannot marry? I long to ask Queen Margaret these questions but I dare not. I dare not show any interest. A queen should be above such gossip. And I may have misunderstood.

I have enough experience of the French court to know that a queen must be circumspect in her dealings with the wives and daughters of important men. Some of them may in the future be my ladies-in-waiting, some may become my friends, some I may never see again if they hardly come to court. I do not know yet which of them will be important to me, because their husbands are important to the king. Some of these women are married to James's closest advisers, some are married to men who would be his enemies if circumstances changed.

I smile equally on them all.

There is to be no bedding ceremony. Instead at a nod from James I slip quietly from the hall. His musicians are playing a galliard with considerable bravura and most of the guests are dancing. My departure will be barely noticed. Marie and Louise follow me. I will not tolerate any raucous jokes, so if any of the matrons present expected to see me to bed, they must needs be disappointed. The Dowager Queen has retired before me, exhausted perhaps with the crowd and an over-indulgence in food.

In the queen's chamber the great high bed of state is hung with embroidered silk and brocades and strewn with flowers. Here the two girls help me to undress and wash the sweat of the heated hall from me. It is done in a subdued near-silence.

They go off to rejoin the dancing and I wait for my new husband. I could envy Marie the carefree courtship of George Seton which she is so obviously enjoying before the reality of marriage and responsibilities overtake her, while I am as nervous as a virgin. I have not long to wait. James slips quietly into the room.

'Mary?'

'My lord.'

'Not here,' he says. He opens the door into the inner chamber and I thankfully throw off the silken quilts of the great state bed and follow him. We pass through to the small private bedroom where my own bed brought from France is more simply dressed. He closes the door behind me and takes me in his arms.

He kisses me gently full on the mouth and pushes me down onto the bed.

'We are both too experienced for coyness,' he says.

I hear the rustle of his clothes, then he climbs naked into the bed beside me and pulls me to him.

He is a matter-of-fact and gentle lover, familiar with the body of a woman. I do not feel any particular joy. This man is still a stranger to me and we do not speak much. I am careful in what I say for I do not know yet what words of mine can amuse or hurt. The formal conversations we have had in the last two days are no guide to his mind.

He quickly falls asleep beside me, while I lie awake, too wrought up by the events of the day to sleep yet. But it relieves me to know that in bed at least I have nothing to worry about, that the connection we must have regularly if there is to be an heir for the throne of Scotland will not be anything to dread.

CHAPTER 3

I stand beside James on the quayside to say farewell to my friends. It is early morning and as we wait the sky becomes lighter. Over in the east the last of the rising sun's pale rays have faded and there are banks of clouds building. Already in the air is the sense of coming autumn.

St Andrews harbour is packed full of trading vessels and fishing boats all busy preparing to catch the tide. We are here to see the French visitors embark. The *Riall* is taking my father and Louise home. She is weeping as she hugs me. She wants to stay, but there are already marriage discussions taking place at Bar-le-Duc and besides, our mother would like her home. Two of my ladies are also going back. They have been homesick and have not settled.

My father has been restless for the last few weeks. It is time he returned to take up his duties. When he took his private leave of me earlier he expressed himself well satisfied with the choice of husband. While no man can compare with his own dear King François, James is everything a king should be, elegant, learned, chivalrous. He is clearly not as rich as François, but then what king is?

I must never forget that while my first duty is to my husband I also have a duty to France and must do everything in my power to strengthen the bonds between the two countries. If there is any matter that the King of France should know then I am to write to my mother.

'What kind of matter?'

'Anything. Above all, any matter that concerns England or Spain.'

There has been a constant stream of messengers between France and Scotland, for even though my father has been granted leave of absence from the court to come here, King François still seeks his advice. There come letters from my mother with instructions for me and offers of help for James. Does he want a new armourer? The French are the best in the world. Gold miners? I had told her there is gold in the king's estates in Eskdale. I pass these messages on to James. He smiles cordially and says, if she would like to send miners then she should, though we do have our own. But yes, he would welcome a French armourer.

'He has not been tested in war,' says my father. 'But I have no doubt he will acquit himself well if ever the occasion comes.'

'I pray it will not.'

He shrugs. All nations must make war at some time or another.

His parting words to my husband are a promise to send some boar. In Scotland the boar is not hunted and he is anxious to introduce James to this sport. The two of them embrace awkwardly and my father boards the ship. The drum beat begins while the rowers take up the rhythm and pull strongly. Soon the *Riall* is well out into the bay and turning south.

David Beaton has already gone. He left last week for France to receive the mitre for his new French bishopric. He has gone eagerly to the consecration, for his duties will be minimal and his income from the diocese substantial. I wonder about his wife and children. They could be acknowledged by the commendator of an abbey who is not in holy orders, but as a Bishop of the Church will he have to deny them?

Gone too is Lord Maxwell, back to his castle of Caerlaverock on the wild marshes of the Solway where he rules, so he told me with pride, over a vast area of barely inhabited bog and mountains, Liddesdale and Nithsdale, haunts of murdering reiving families, a land where no one knows where Scotland ends and England begins. Him, I will not miss.

Now as the ships drop out of sight, the activity on the quayside resumes.

I feel bereft. Marie moves forward and squeezes my hand, but already I know that her thoughts are with Lord Seton, who is standing over against the spice warehouse with others of the king's gentlemen.

Oliver Sinclair pulls at James's sleeve, they step aside and Sinclair murmurs something I cannot hear.

'Will you stay with me today?' I ask, but already James is moving away.

'The weather will break soon. We will take the hawks out.'

'Cannot I come?' No one had said anything about hunting today.

'Best not. Just in case.' He glances at my belly, smiles slightly and strides off up the hill towards the palace, the men running after him, leaving me to follow with my ladies. I am not pregnant. Even if I were, there would be no danger in riding. Am I to be coddled like a sick calf? Marie comes back to my side.

I look round to gather up the ladies. 'A walk round the town,' I decide. 'The exercise will be good for us.'

The townspeople have become accustomed to us. There is something marvellous in their determination not to show any awe or subservience to the court. They ignore us, the women with children on their hips, the men unloading carts, and all pursuing their own business affairs. I reflect that now the French visitors have gone my true business as a queen will begin and I too will no doubt have tasks to perform. This cheers me in a small way. I will soon be useful to James.

A group of pilgrims stand aside as we pass, in the middle of them a child on a litter being carried by two boys not much older. They hardly see us, intent as they are on joining the long queue waiting to enter the cathedral. Their purpose is to pray to the bones of the blessed Apostle Andrew to cure whatever ails the boy.

My purpose is to hide my sorrow at the departure of my family. I lead the ladies towards the quieter Church of the Holy Trinity. Maître Guillet recites the paternoster. I hear his voice break and he pauses. I wonder whether as he watched the ships leave he wished he, too, were going home.

On the way back to the palace we pass by St Salvator's College where the scholars are lounging outside in the sunshine. More than one of them nods to Maître Guillet. So he is making friends. I am glad.

In the state rooms the servants are already dismantling the tapestries and rolling them up, for we are to move on to Falkland Palace the day after tomorrow. They pay us no heed. In my own quarters the chamber women are helping the wardrobe mistress pack up my clothes.

We dine quietly for the hall is not crowded. Most of the lords who came for the wedding celebrations have returned to their estates.

'I won't come to you tonight,' James says to me softly. 'It has been difficult for you today, saying goodbye to your father and friends. I will leave you in peace.'

I do not want to be left in peace. I want to be held in his arms and comforted, but I do not know how to say this. Presently James excuses himself. His gentlemen follow him out, some to join him in his privy chamber, some to the stables. They bow to me as they leave. Oliver Sinclair's bow is deepest but he is smirking. Lord Seton throws a backward glance at Marie. I am left with the women. The servants hover, waiting for the evening to end so that they can start packing the boards away.

In my privy chamber I dismiss the maids and signal to Marie that she is to stay. I take off the new jewelled cap which is a present from James. It is too tight and will have to be adjusted. Marie unpins my hair and runs her fingers through it, shaking it free.

'Headache?'

'A little. Is Seton waiting for you?'

'Let him wait.'

'Marie . . . ' I hesitate, but I need to know. There has been a question at the back of my mind for weeks, ever since my conversation with Queen Margaret. I have watched and waited, but since I cannot ask James I know no more than I did then. 'Does Seton ever mention a woman, Lord Erskine's daughter?'

She is massaging the back of my head with her thumbs. I close my eyes and wait.

Finally: 'The one that's married to Robert Douglas of Lochleven?'

'Is she?'

Another pause. 'She has a son by the king. Do you mean that one?'

'Yes, I suppose I mean that one. Does Seton ever mention her?'

'No, why should he? There is more than one woman with a bastard.'

After she has gone, I dismiss the chamber child to the alcove outside the room where she sleeps. If James does not want me, I want no one else near me tonight. I blow out all the candles save one. From the kist I take out the box where my letters are kept. I read again the one that James sent me, the one where he expresses his need for a helpmeet to govern the kingdom. I reach for the letters from Louis, but I hesitate to lift them. I draw my hand back and close the box. The past is done with.

THE FRENCH VISITORS were entertained with tourneys where the knights and gentlemen, French and Scottish, could show off their courage, strength and chivalry. Now, as we settle into a routine at court there is less of this, though the young men continue to train while the old men teach them. Skill in the field and in the saddle is as much a training for war as for pleasure.

In Paris the chivalry of the joust spills over into the chivalry of the court, and every woman has her cavalier sighing over her and writing love poetry. In the tilt every knight wears hidden or openly the favour of his lady. The men and the women circle each other in a courtly dance. The days are long and the nights warm, the wine is strong and the perfume of the roses is heady. The courtly dance can become less chaste.

As companion to the king's daughters and lady-in-waiting to the queen I was often at the heart of this, but my heart was never in it. As long as I was a virgin I was safe but any married woman who remained at court and who was the least bit willing was considered fair prey to be seduced with words. I was glad when my marriage to Louis took me away from the court and I could spend most of my days at Chateaudun. When his duties in the service of the king required that I too be at court I did my best to hold myself aloof.

Now as the gallants display their skill I see that in James's court the chivalric code is as highly regarded as it is in France. On the tilting ground the jousting is not less dangerous, nor the swordplay less skilful. The horses are as heavy, the lances as long and the competition as fierce, but the heady sensuousness of the French court does not translate to the cooler air of Scotland. I am glad.

There is poetry written and love songs sung, but the smooth, charming ripple of compliments that a Frenchwoman will hear from her knight do not come easily to the lips of the Scotsmen. I observe tentative courtships between the Scots and my French ladies but these are serious matters, not a prelude to casual seduction.

I can say these things to Sir David Lyndsay. When at last I meet him I like him immediately. His smile is that of a man happy in his life and not the

71

automatic smile of the courtier, though he is that too. As Snowdon Herald and Depute Lord Lyon he has responsibility for all matters of chivalry, from the practical design of coats of arms for those entitled to wear them, to the order of precedence at every court function, to the rules of the joust. He knows the French court for he has been there many times as James's envoy. Now he is as old as my father and his travels are in the past. His age and gentle charm let me confide these thoughts to him.

'Bear in mind,' says Sir David. 'That the conduct of the court comes from the top. There has not been a woman at the head of the Scottish court for almost the whole of the king's lifetime, and the gentler arts a lady will bring have been in abeyance. The queen sets the tone. The ladies will take their lead from you, and the men will take their lead from the ladies.'

Sir David has a private face and a public face. The public man entertains the court with poetry and song, and he obviously takes great pleasure in organising the masques that exhaust the energies of the young squires and pages in the evening.

The private face I have glimpsed and as we become accustomed to one another I see it more often. There is a deep affection between James and Sir David. They glance at one another when something amuses them. James will casually pat the shoulder of the older man in passing. Sometimes they speak together in half-sentences as though each could finish the thought of the other. It is an intimacy I can envy.

'He was a father to me,' says James.

Sir David is preparing an armorial which will be the definitive record of the arms of all the noble and

72

knightly families in Scotland and to which my own arms are being added.

'Should I attempt to learn them all?'

'It would do no harm, if you have the inclination. The major ones you must know. And it would be as well for you to be able to differentiate at sight who are the king's friends and who are his enemies. There are, for instance,' and he pulls several of the coloured sheets, 'branches of the Douglas family who are in exile and will never be allowed back into Scotland as long as James lives. There are others who are his loyal and trusted servants.'

There is so much to learn and most of it has to be discovered from chasing wisps and hints. I can memorise who is a son or a brother of whom, but there is nothing to tell me who is at enmity with his cousin or which branch of which family has been feuding with a neighbour for generations while other branches of the same families are allies. I feel in despair sometimes. I make a joke of it, but Sir David seeks to reassure me.

'Many of the quarrels blow hot and blow cool again. Most are about land and many are resolved by the king, for he has learned wisdom in these matters and will stand no nonsense from his lords. He is a man who knows how to balance one against another. He had to learn from a very young age.'

THERE ARE FEWER courtiers now that the celebrations for our marriage are ended. The people around the king are those with official business. Gavin Dunbar, the Chancellor, Keeper of the Great Seal, is often with James. He is Archbishop of Glasgow and has the reputation of being a harsh persecutor of

73

protestants, with, I am told, a splendid talent for the formal cursing of all who fail to pay their dues to the Church. James introduces him as his old mentor and guardian.

'Between him and Davie Lyndsay I learned everything I know.'

'Your Grace, we thought we were teaching him but he was learning for himself the kingly arts of diplomacy. When one of us said nay he would run to the other and persuade him to say yea. I had not these grey hairs till I had the care of him and I have had them ever since.'

His words are light and sound kindly but there is a coldness in his eye as he looks at me. I have seen this same wariness in some of the others of the king's advisers. Do they fear I will usurp their role?

There are those who already feel like old comfortable friends. Bishop David Beaton is the Keeper of the Privy Seal. It seems to me many of the men about the king and his council are churchmen, and I comment on this.

'They serve me well,' says James. 'There is mutual goodwill because there is a mutual purpose, to make Scotland prosperous.'

The king is determined that all of Scotland will be peaceful under his rule and to this end we must make regular progresses round the country, not only to be seen but to dispense justice and settle disputes, of which there seem to be many amongst neighbouring magnates. To begin with I will go with him, for he must show off his bride, but soon, God willing, my condition will be such that I will be able to remain peaceably in one place, probably Falkland Palace, which is where James will spend what days of leisure he has, where we can be more private and where there will be less ceremonial. That is the plan.

And so my new life begins.

MY MOTHER WRITES that an envoy of King Henry of England has been touring through France. He stopped at Bar-le-Duc and then went on to Nancy.

'He had a painter with him. My mother thinks they are secretly making portraits of every girl they meet who might be a suitable bride for King Henry. You know that Louise was suggested, but of course she is much too young. They are thinking of my cousin now.'

'My poor Uncle Henry,' says James. 'I have plucked the finest of the ladies from under his nose and none of sense will have him. He must scratch around as best he can.'

Our laughter is drowned out by the outriders sounding their horns to signal our approach to Linlithgow Palace.

'It is my favourite,' says James. 'It is where I was born.'

Already on this progress the places we have stayed have become a blur in my mind. We have spent several weeks moving from palace to castle to palace, for not only must James show off his bride to his people, he must show off his palaces to me. Which palace had the new frieze of gold and blue in the presence chamber? Was it Falkland, or was it the old king's palace at Stirling? The great hall at Stirling has the high roof beams of an upturned boat, but which room had the ceiling bosses showing heroes from antiquity? Holyrood was cold.

The familiar tapestries travel with us and I still have my own bed, but so much is new, new to the king as well as to me, for he is buying great Turkey carpets, glass from Murano, the finest linen from the Low Countries for our household use, wall hangings from Milan, leather from Spain. His agents abroad have instructions to seek out the best silver tableware and from time to time gold, enamelled and jewelled pieces are delivered for the royal chapels and our private oratories.

Already difficulties are arising about accommodation. James's palaces are large, but fitting in my own people, several hundred of them, alongside his is causing friction. There are my horses and mules and all the grooms and stable lads, while my cooks and pâtissières must have their own kitchens. M. de Curel comes to me sometimes in despair. Where to put all the people? Building work goes on constantly but the space is no sooner ready than it is filled.

It is in high spirits that we approach the palace of Linlithgow. My exclamation of pleasure at the sight of it is genuine. Against the setting sun I see a towered, turreted palace, a palace of enchantment glowing golden beside the still waters of a lake.

At the top of the Kirkgait James reigns in his horse and points out the new gateway.

'The design is my own.'

The panels above the gateway are bright with new paint.

'That one shows the arms of the Order of the Garter. My Uncle Henry was good enough to bestow that on me three years ago. We had signed a new treaty of peace between Scotland and England.'

'Does it still exist, this treaty?'

'Yes. It will last till a year after the death of whichever one of us dies first. And since my uncle is twice my age I think we need not be troubled by war with England.'

'I am glad of that.'

'War is foolish. It empties the treasury.' His voice is suddenly harsh and I have nothing to say. It was war with Henry that killed his father. He does not talk of it.

Behind us I can hear the restless movement of horses and riders as the cavalcade waits for us to move. But the king must not be hurried.

'The next panel?' I ask.

'That is our own Order of the Thistle, then comes the Order of the Golden Fleece. I received that from Spain. At the time there were negotiations for a marriage with one of the Emperor Charles's kin, but that came to nothing. The fourth is the Order of St Michael. That is the most precious to me since it was bestowed by King François.'

Of course it was, when he was marrying a princess of France.

We ride through the pend slowly for I must crane my neck to admire the bright carvings over our heads of the beasts of the royal arms. A unicorn stands upright at one side and on the other a lion. There is a winged deer of France, put there for Madeleine.

The Keeper of the Palace and all his people are waiting for us in the Inner Close.

'Sir James Hamilton of Finnart.' James introduces him. 'My most valued servant. He has been in charge of the building work here.'

Hamilton of Finnart is a heavy man in middle age, not tall, and the impression he gives is of solidness, sturdiness. His hair is grey but his cheeks are plump and smooth.

As we follow him James says to me in a low voice, 'Finnart is the half-brother of the Earl of Arran, but they are not friends.' I understand. Though most of the men in James's court are related to one another, blood does not always breed affection.

In the centre of the courtyard is a great edifice surrounded by scaffolding.

'This will be the largest and the best fountain in all of Scotland, aye and England too. It will soon be finished.'

'We have suspended work, Your Grace, so that you are not disturbed by the noise,' says Finnart.

Already in place are the life-size figures of the unicorn and one of a lion and several gryphons, and circling all at every level there are intricate patterns of squares and rings. The heads which will spout the water are already in place on the edges of the basin and there will be another basin above that, supported by statues, all still to be finished.

'It will flow constantly with water piped down from the hills, but we can cut off the water and use wine instead when there are special celebrations.'

After the welcoming feast in the Great Hall James calls for silence. He signals to an usher, who cries out the name 'Sir James Hamilton of Finnart'.

'Come forward James Hamilton,' he repeats.

James stands up and signals for silence. 'James Hamilton,' he says. 'Your work is most pleasing to us and to our new queen. Take this for your reward.' He hands Finnart a bag of coin. 'So will be rewarded all who serve their king faithfully. And I appoint you as Master for all our building work.'

Finnart bows and retreats. There will be more rewards of course, less publicly given. The bag of gold coin, valuable as it is, is also symbolic. The estates which have already been awarded to him are extensive and lucrative. Master of Works is only the latest of the posts which he has held under James.

We settle comfortably into Linlithgow. My suite of rooms is the largest and finest I have yet had and I now have my own audience chamber where petitioners come every day seeking favours or help. James has given me some advisers, and I need these, for though I am learning the language quickly I still have difficulty with the speech of many of the people.

These advisers murmur in my ear the answer to the pleas. This one can be referred to my almoner, that one must take his petition to the king himself. The lady whose husband is in prison must appeal to the justices, the man with the complaint about his neighbour must be spoken to sharply, for he is a regular troublemaker. I do not enjoy these occasions, but I am learning the duties of a queen. Some pleas are easier. This one has a son who has a way with birds and wishes to train as a falconer, that one has a daughter old enough to enter the royal service as a maid. A word with M. de Curel and the child is offered a trial. Sometimes I catch his sigh. More people to be housed and fed, but I smile and gently scold him. We have so much and so many people have so little.

I receive a long letter from my mother. My son has scurvy. My sister Louise has been ill with congestion of the lungs and a fever, but is recovering. My other siblings have had the bloody flux but they are now well. I feel a panic rising within me. The people I love are ill and may die and I may never see them again. I may never see my mother or France again. When I open the Book of Hours every page reminds me of my grandmother. I feel a physical ache in my heart and confess to Maître Guillet the sin of discontent. He imposes a light penance and absolves me. We both pretend this will quiet the yearnings.

FROM TIME TO TIME James does not appear in the hall, sending word that he is ill. I send anxious enquiries back but am told that he prefers to be alone, that he will be well tomorrow and not to fret. But as time passes and I note that the day after his absence there is no sign of illness and he seems much as usual, I begin to suspect that these absences have less to do with illness and more to do with – what? I do not frame to myself my suspicions. We have been married such a short time. I am still feeling my way among these strangers.

One evening after I have presided in state but without James. when the candles are burning low and the people are beginning to drift away, I return to my own quarters. I dismiss the maids, telling them to return later as I wish to sit for a while. When they have gone I slip out of my chamber and make my way by the private stair to James's room. I quietly open his door and push aside the curtain. I start back in shock, for there are two beggars there, lounging in the flickering firelight, drinking wine. Then as my eyes become accustomed to the dimness I see that the men in drab clothing, almost in rags, are James himself and Oliver Sinclair.

'My lord.'

James leaps to his feet, but Sinclair continues to sit. I wait for James to reprimand him for his insolence, but he does not. James appears to be intoxicated, though that is not one of his weaknesses.

'Ah Mary, you have found my secret.'

'Why are you dressed in those old clothes?'

He laughs and I realise he is in an exuberant mood which has nothing to do with wine. 'We have been out on the town, have we not, Oliver.'

Sinclair nods, eyeing me complacently.

'Doing what? Why?'

'To walk among my people, of course. To listen to them. To joke with them about the iniquities of the king and his court.'

'They do not know you?'

'Of course they do not know me.'

'My lord, it is undignified.'

His smile fades. 'Nothing a king does is ever undignified.'

It is on the tip of my tongue to say that King François would never do something so demeaning, but something in James's eyes tells me this would be a criticism too far.

I turn away. Oliver Sinclair hastily leaps to his feet with a gesture as if he intends to open the door for me, but I am too quick for him, as perhaps he intended me to be.

We do not talk of it again. James continues from time to time to absent himself in the evenings without explanation.

LEARNING THE LIMITS of my queenly role is painful.

'My lord, may I have a word?'

He nods, but his gaze strays back to the plans which are spread on the bench in front of him. By his side Finnart bows his head briefly to acknowledge me. The head gardener Morrison stands by with a scowl black as thunder. I see what is amiss. The area James and Finnart are looking at is where his most tender plants, carefully brought from warmer climates, grow within sheltering walls.

'See here,' says James waving his hand. 'This whole area is to be the new tennis court.' It is the latest sport. He wants to be able to play it at every one of his palaces.

He glances at the letter in my hand. 'What is it?' he asks. 'Does aught ail your family?'

'No, nothing like that.'

He draws me aside, out of the hearing of the men.

'This is from my uncle the Cardinal of Lorraine. He says you have in prison a man called Hugh Campbell. Do you?'

'Perhaps. What is it to your uncle?'

'He has been approached by friends of this man Campbell to have him released so that he may return to France. He asks me to speak to you about it.'

'And does the cardinal your uncle tell you why Campbell is in prison, or why he should be released, other than that certain gentlemen have an interest in him?'

'No.' I become aware of the coldness in his voice and falter. He is tapping his fingers against his thigh. 'No. No, he does not give any detail.'

'Well, I would suggest that the cardinal should look after the affairs of his church and leave me to mind the affairs of my kingdom. And it ill becomes you to act as a messenger in matters you do not understand.'

He turns away and a moment later is bending over the plans of the new tennis court, asking Finnart questions.

I feel myself beginning to tremble. I stand, not daring to move in case I stumble. If the others have sharp hearing they may have heard. Morrison stands by. He may not have understood the words, for we spoke in French, as we always do privately, but he must at least have caught the tone. Suddenly he gives me a brief small smile and I am angry, angry with him for his sympathy and angry with myself for incurring it.

I take a deep breath and steady myself and turn and walk calmly away, signalling to my women who have been waiting by the summer house, calling them to keep up.

When we meet again later in the day, James is as amiable as ever. Nothing more is said and will not be said, not by me, not by James but I realise I must be more circumspect in the future.

Some days later Marie, more free to gossip than I can ever be, hears that Hugh Campbell has been released and has gone to France. It was, apparently, a quarrel with another lord in Ayrshire, a story of money owed and murder done. The king resolved the matter in his own way. A substantial fine makes its way into the royal coffers. Campbell is released and the aggrieved lord has been amply compensated with Campbell lands.

My uncle writes and thanks me for my intervention. I do not reply.

IT IS NOT ONLY I who can misjudge James's mood. Bishop David Beaton, heavier and sleeker, comes to him with pride glowing from him like a furnace.

'The Holy Father has seen fit to offer me a cardinal's hat.'

'Indeed.' James marks with his finger the line in the book he is reading, but the bishop will not be deflated.

'It is a great honour for Scotland.'

'But I did not seek this honour,' says James and there is puzzlement in his voice. 'Why should the Pope show such favour?'

'It is a recognition of Scotland's fight against the heresies despoiling Europe.'

'Or perhaps for your services to the King of France. You are, after all, one of his bishops.'

James has closed his book, and his fingers are going tap, tap, tap on the cover.

'I always act in the interests of Scotland.'

'And in the interests of David Beaton.'

Beaton is at a loss to answer and can only shake his head and make fluttering gestures with his hands, as if he would bless James.

'And when is the consecration to take place?'

'The Holy Father says I need not travel all the way to Rome. It can be done in Antwerp.'

'You are honoured indeed.'

'But as to when, only when you can spare me to make the journey.'

'I can hardly prevent you travelling on Church business. Mind this, Davie, your first loyalty is to Scotland, not to Rome and not to France.'

'You don't need to say that.'

'I have said it.' James picks up his book again, and the bishop, dismissed, bows himself out.

When the door has closed behind him James starts to laugh.

'James?'

He reaches into the drawer of his desk and pulls out several letters. 'From Cardinal Farnese,' he says, tossing one aside. Another: 'From Ferrerio, the papal nuncio in France. All congratulating me and praising me for a true and loyal son of the Church.'

'You already knew?'

'David Beaton forgets I have my own envoys in Rome that do not depend on him or his people.'

'Are you angry?'

'It will be useful to have a cardinal. I can tweak the Pope's purse strings the more effectively.'

He pushes the letters back out of sight. 'I will answer these tomorrow and assure all of them of my delight.' He picks up his book again and soon he is absorbed.

He had looked so terrifyingly angry he even cowed the bishop. How real are the flashes to anger he displays? If his temper is feigned, what of his apparent good moods? Perhaps there is a carapace about him that he can shift and adjust as the need demands it. Perhaps what I see is only the outer shell, the pretence put on to face the world.

THIS I HAVE in common with the new Cardinal Beaton: the fight against heresy. I have not forgotten the words of my grandmother. *Perhaps God has a purpose for you.* If this is my purpose then I will do my best to fulfil God's will. No heretical literature shall damage the Church here as it has done elsewhere. Books are printed abroad and smuggled into Scotland. Pamphlet after pamphlet denying the truth of Holy Scripture pour from the printing presses abroad. This trade must be stopped. The legislation against it is constantly renewed and the punishment for being in possession is horrific.

James seems to have little interest in it. He hunches his shoulders when I try to talk to him about it.

'More promptings from your uncle the cardinal?'

I assure him not. It is the duty of all good Christian people to defend the Church against the evangelicals who would destroy it.

Beaton waxes voluble on the subject. 'The books are coming in through the Low Countries. I will put a stop to it, in God's name I will.'

'In God's name, or Beaton's name?' asks James.

'Of course, there is no profit in it,' flashes back Beaton, and for a moment there is stillness as Beaton realises he has gone too far, but he is able to continue smoothly, 'though there is great favour with the Pope and we become part of the great defence against the heresies of King Henry.' This is the right thing to say. James is ever watchful for ways in which he can score against his uncle.

WITH THE SPRING we celebrate the first anniversary of our marriage.

My mother's letters are becoming more anxious. Always in one form or another the question, Do you have good news for us yet? And every month I have to acknowledge that no, I do not have good news for anyone.

As summer comes we travel to Edinburgh to observe the obsequies for the anniversary of the death of Queen Madeleine. She has been dead for two years.

The chapel of Holyrood is draped in black. By my side James barely moves, save occasionally to cover his face with his hand. The Archbishop of St Andrews leads a full day of mourning. The archbishop is old and shaky and often has to retire to rest and the younger men take over, among them Cardinal Beaton, who shows little sign of sorrow and instead appears to be relishing the occasion. As the choristers sing the interminable requiem mass I reflect what a silly girl Madeleine was. There is more dignity and grace in this memorial service for her than ever there was in her life.

The women here are eager to tell me that the match between her and James was a true love match. Another French bride had been chosen for the king, but as soon as he saw Madeleine he rejected the other. I know that story. I can only guess at the feelings of the rejected girl, but she has been lost in the romance of the story.

I knew Madeleine in the brief period when I was at court as one of the companions to the king's daughters, before my marriage. She was a pretty girl, slight of build, with wide eyes, a soft voice and hands that were forever touching and stroking the sleeves of the gentlemen. She feigned that helpless air that seems to appeal to even the most intelligent of men, and James was fooled along with the rest.

It was she who was determined to have him, or his crown more likely. There was no stopping her and she tormented her father King François for his consent until he gave way. Her stepmother was indifferent, and perhaps eager to have the precocious, sickly girl away from the court. It was clear that Madeleine would not survive long. She had already coughed up blood. She ordered the maids to keep quiet about this under pain of death, but some of her ladies knew.

King's daughter she may have been, but she would have been a poor, useless queen. I have already in my short time here learned to listen to this lord and that lord who seek favours from the king, but only to listen and promise nothing. Madeleine would have charmed them all and each one would believe himself specially favoured and they would be set at one another's head. No, a court with Madeleine as its queen would not have been a peaceful place. *Requiescat in pace*, Madeleine. I keep these thoughts to myself and murmur the responses with the rest of the mourning congregation.

ON WET AFTERNOONS when we sit together, the Scotswomen who now form part of my court murmur to each other in rapid undertones. I now know the language fairly well but when a woman has to keep all her wits about her it is expedient that people think she does not understand what they are saying, for then they say things which can be useful.

Or hurtful.

The women by the fireplace stitching an altar cloth are speculating whether, if Madeleine had lived, there would now be a boy in the nursery. I play the ten of spades and take the pot, and say in a cheerful voice 'What are you saying? Translate please.' And they flutter and give me some salacious gossip about the English court, with which they seem to have a fascination.

It hurts. It hurts but I do not show it.

James asks me if aught is amiss. I assure him all is well. Am I content? Yes. What do I miss most about Chateaudun? I tell him nothing, I have everything I need here for happiness, but he presses me. He will order a portrait made in France of my boy there so that I can see how he has grown. I tell him I am grateful.

We are standing before the paintings which M. Corneille made of me, and the other which he made of James when James was in Paris to marry Madeleine. Unlike me, James was not looking at the artist. He looks thoughtful, his mind clearly on other things.

Every monarch in Europe is having his portrait painted but none more so than Henry of England. He has fine artists in his employ, artists who are given the task of rendering into paint all the great men of the court, and more and more the king himself and his family. It is said he has become so obsessed he even has them painting group portraits that include those members of the family who are dead, as if this would bring them back to life. And François too has invited Italian artists to his court and rewards them well.

'Why do we have no such skilled men in Scotland,' wonders James. 'I will remedy that.' He makes enquiries and finds someone. The man is commissioned to paint a double portrait of James and myself.

When the new portrait is done and put on display, Marie stands in front of it shaking her head.

'You are right. It is not very good but do not say anything.' I tell her. 'We would not want to hurt the man's feelings. I know I do not look like that.' The artist has made me look thin and gaunt.

Marie looks from me to the portrait. 'If you are not careful you will.'

And of course she has seen what I have been reluctant to admit. The courtly pursuits, while pleasant, do not satisfy me. I need more. At Chateaudun I was used to running the estate while my husband was away and there are always matters on which they consult me. My mother writes that a trusted servant has died, who shall have his place? A court action involving my son's estate looks to be settled soon. But she only tells me these things as a matter of courtesy. She does not need my advice. All the decisions have been taken by the time the letters reach me. What can I do save write back and say do as you think fit?

Here, I have no such responsibility. Once I have gone over my household accounts with M. du Fou and worried about the seemingly endless expenditure there is no work for me.

I press James to allow me to help him. He declines with a smile. He has all the help he needs. He has secretaries a-plenty. He does not think his Uncle Henry of England or François need use their wives as scribes.

'I was not thinking of merely scribing. Can you not talk to me about the difficulties, the decisions to be made?'

'Such matters are not for women. You will have work enough when there are bairns in the nursery.' Thus he dismisses the matter.

I would like to remind him that he wrote to me, being in need of a wife who would be a partner in the great enterprise of government and not just a decorative queen or a breeder of sons, but I say nothing and leave it be, for I have not fulfilled even the minimum requirement of a queen: that of conceiving a child.

A LETTER COMES by special messenger from his mother, Queen Margaret. She is full of complaints about the way she is kept short of money and begging him once again not to block the divorce from her third husband.

He drops the letter in the fire.

'It was hard for her,' I say.

'You were not there.'

'I can imagine how it was. She was a young woman left as regent. She had to learn to govern quickly.'

'She was foolish,' he says.

'Foolish because she was ignorant. What experience did she have of governing a kingdom, a young woman brought up to nothing but pleasure and idleness?'

He whistles to his dogs then and strides from the room. I work off my annoyance by walking my ladies round and round the garden till they express themselves worn out.

NOW IT IS EVENING and time for James to relax. My musicians in the gallery are playing some new music come lately from Italy. James is playing chess with Cardinal Beaton. Oliver Sinclair is behind him, with his arm about the king's shoulders, looking on, occasionally glancing over at David Lyndsay as much as to say, *See, I am the one closest to the king.* Lyndsay turns his back. George Seton is standing in a window embrasure with Marie, but even as I look at them, George glances over towards James to see if he is wanted. There is Sir Tom Bellenden, the king's secretary, deep in conversation with Sir John Borthwick. These two are known to sympathise with the evangelists who preach the reformed religion. That may be what they are discussing now. James permits such freedoms. I do not like it but when I have ventured to express my disquiet he merely shrugs it off. They are good servants, he says, and it is better to know what men are thinking because then we can be aware of danger before it is upon us.

Near me young Tom Erskine is reminiscing with the latest visitor to the court, Giovanni Ferrerio, of his time at the university of Padua. Others are playing cards, or talking in groups in low voices. Two young pages are demonstrating dance steps to two of my maids in waiting. I keep an eye on these to make sure they do not overstep the boundary of decorum, but the boys too are alert in case the king wants something. Their fathers are important men in the north and service at the court is a step on the road to manhood and power. Young as they are, they know where their duty lies.

Tonight they are all relaxing. Tomorrow morning these same men will be in the council chamber discussing the latest news from Spain, from France, from the Low Countries. They will decide the next move in Scotland's foreign policy. Later on they will talk of new regulations for trading. On other days some of these men will sit as judges in the Court of Session to hear the pleas of the common people.

The same men will take to the lists with James in preparation for the next tournament or they will be practising at the butts. When they go hawking, or when they rest on a hillside waiting for sight of the deer, a man will be by the king's side with a murmured remark about the situation in the northern islands, or about a rumour of sedition in the west, or with second thoughts about a council decision. Men like these are always with the king.

I am set apart with my ladies. My only function is to bear children and any woman can do that. I could do more if only he would let me. The hope I felt surging me when I read his letter to me, the letter in which he asked me to be his helpmeet, the companion by his side, has all but died. I am hardly ever by his side now, save on state occasions and the formal evenings we spend with the court, and these are so public he and I might be strangers to one another.

I determine to speak to him about this, but even as I make up my mind I know my courage will fail me and I will say nothing.

CHAPTER 4

How can I write to my mother that I am unhappy?

How can I write that I am cold all the time, despite the furs and the wool that hangs heavily round my shoulders, that the sunshine is pale and that everything, all the time, seems to be moist to the touch? That there are days when the rain falls relentlessly and everyone is surly and quarrelsome?

Instead I write about the changing colours of the countryside as the seasons turn, about the clouds that swirl and romp across the sky, about the astonishing colours in the sky at dawn, about the rainbows.

How can I write that I yearn to see my son and hold him in my arms?

Instead I write about the marriages that are beginning to take place between my people and the Scots and the babies being born who are becoming like a family to me.

How can I write that I feel crushed by the constant presence of people, of how I am never alone, that everywhere I am attended by my ladies, who must never leave my side, by courtiers seeking favours, posts for this cousin or that, for alms for their charities. I do not say that every detail of my diet and my health are common gossip and that the bleeding is every month known about and sighed over.

Instead I write about the songs and poetry that are a constant pleasure on the wet afternoons and long evenings, for this is a court that is full of musicians and storytellers.

How can I write about the ache in my heart to see my homeland?

How can I write that I am lonely?

THE LAST NOTE of the viols quivers in the air and the listeners sigh and stir and applaud. I signal to M. Columbell that they should pause now, for David Lyndsay is to entertain us with his new poem.

'It acknowledges the influence of Her Grace on the lives of our women. If Your Grace will permit?'

'Of course,' I say.

He clears his throat, bows to James, 'Sire,' and begins.

'Sire, though Your Grace has put great order
Both in the High Land and the Border
Yet may I make a supplication
To have some reformation . . .

He pauses and there is a wary silence of anticipation in the room. His views on the Church are known. Surely he will not speak of that in such a light-hearted tone. Then he moves smoothly on:

Sovereign, I speak of side tails
Which throw up dust and muddy trails
Three quarters long behind their heels.

There is laughter now, for we have heard Sir David lament this before, the overlong trains which the women of Edinburgh are wearing on their gowns in imitation of the court ladies.

It is all very well for queens – here he bows in my direction - to wear long trains, for they have ladies to hold them up, and bishops – he bows to the cardinal – for they have men to perform the same service, but what is to be done about the burgesses' wives who wear in the street gowns more suited to the ballroom and every little strumpet parades long side tails to their petticoats that pick up mud and worse from the streets? What is to be done? Warming to his theme he begins to rant.

When moorland Meg that milks the yowes
In barn nor byre she willna bide
Withoot her tails beside.

The poem becomes both earthy and bawdy and the older women shake their heads and smile and my young ladies drop their eyes and blush as the hall explodes with laughter. I am careful to hide my irritation. In conversation the language would be unseemly. It is not less unacceptable because it is in verse, but I will not offend Sir David.

He finishes with a flourish in the direction of James with a plea to ban the fashions. James applauds with the others and shakes his head.

"'Tis beyond me, Davie. When did ever legislation give a woman common sense?"

When the dancing has started I signal Sir David to come and sit by me. He looks at me sideways, as if expecting a scolding.

'Is it seemly for a poet to write of such earthy matters?'

'I write what I see.'

'It is true our French fashions do not translate well into the wet, muddy, soggy country that Scotland is.'

'Nay, you cannot blame the weather.'

'And the side tails are not so very long.'

'A poet is allowed some exaggeration.'

'If you wish to improve people's behaviour I wonder you do not write about the saints.'

'Why would I do that, Your Grace?'

'It would both entertain and instruct.'

'I hope I do both, writing about those who still live, with all their frailties.'

'The convent where I was educated was dedicated to the memory of St Clare, the sister of St Francis. She would make a suitable subject for one of your poems, or even an Interlude.'

'Of course. Our painters would enjoy creating a forest with beasts peering from the trees, or a mountain top with birds flying round, but if I know women, Your Grace, the Lady Clare would shoo them away for fear they become entangled in her hair.'

'You demean my sex.'

'Nay, Your Grace, I admire your sex greatly. But I cannot think that the saints were saintly all the time. They were but human. Until they died and had gone beyond life's temptations.'

'You hold such matters lightly?'

'I would not wish to instruct anyone in the ways of the saints.'

'Do you agree then with the new learning that appealing for the aid of saints has no purpose?'

I see Maître Guillet sitting near us and from the tilt of his head I know he is listening to our conversation.

Sir David is weighing up my question. 'I am no Lutheran if that is what Your Grace wishes to know. They go too far. But I can read the arguments which come from them.'

'I have no wish to probe,' I say quietly. Even to read the heretical works is punishable now, but David Lyndsay is so favoured by the king that no enquiry could touch him. He does not hide his opinions, but then neither does he flaunt them.

'I am not blind to the abuses of the Church and the pursuit of wealth with the claim that the saints can shorten the time of our loved ones in purgatory is shameful,' he says.

Maître Guillet becomes aware I have seen him and begins to move away, as if embarrassed to be found listening.

'Maître Guillet,' I call. 'Do you agree with Sir David?'

'I have not Sir David's learning.'

I look at him curiously. He has become very silent lately, not his usual self. I wonder if he is yearning for France. He is not often seen in the company of the men of the court. Perhaps he too is lonely.

Cardinal Beaton, wealthiest of all the churchmen in Scotland, is sitting beside the king and they are laughing at some joke. The poem contained little barbs touching on the vanity of churchmen, but such remarks slide off the cardinal as rain on a window pane.

'The saints themselves are not responsible for the use that men make of them,' says Maître Guillet.

'There is none can say for sure the saints are responsible for anything,' murmurs Sir David.

There is a pause and Maître Guillet takes the opportunity to bow to me and walk out of the hall. He clearly does not wish to debate with Sir David.

I pursue my purpose. 'I have heard that here in Scotland lived a saint who answers the prayers of barren women.' It is out.

'Every land has such.' But he is quick to understand and there is compassion in his voice. 'St Adrian has a shrine on an island out in the estuary of the river. It is not easy to reach. It needs good weather. The monks there, the keepers of the shrine, have turned their backs on the world.'

'Like my Poor Clares.'

'The boatmen who take pilgrims there do very well from . . .' he hesitates for a moment and I believe he was about to say from the superstition of women. But he continues, 'from the longings of women.'

But he and I both know that my need is beyond longing, it has become a matter of the protection of the king's throne. We look up as a braying laugh echoes round the hall, drowning out the music. Young Lord Arran, a thin young man, recently come into his title, is the centre of a group round the fireplace, no doubt telling some tale of bravado, for that is the nature of his talk. I have observed that he is generally not well liked, but if James does not sire a legitimate child, Arran is next in the line of succession for the throne. I remember the hungry way his wife regarded me as we dined on my wedding day.

Sir David Lyndsay has no children. I wonder about his wife. Did she ever pray to St Adrian? Would Sir David know if she had? She is past the age of childbearing. I do not know her, for she lives quietly and is never at court. She was once the king's principal embroiderer, but I hear that her hands are now twisted and painful.

As the evening ends the king catches my eye and gives me the signal that he will come to me tonight. Perhaps there will be no need for St Adrian.

MY DEAR MARIE is married to Lord George Seton. The wedding is exuberant and joyous for all concerned, not least for his children, the oldest three of whom have been brought to attend and who eye their new stepmother with something like awe as she crouches beside them to listen to their childish chatter and pulls droll faces to make them laugh.

When she takes her leave of me in the privacy of my chambers she hangs round my neck and swears that she will be my eternal friend and her marriage will make no difference. Seton must return to the court after their wedding trip, for he is one of James's most trusted old friends, and she will come with him. I know that her pregnancies will keep her away but that is for the future and for now I hug her and agree that I cannot do without her for long.

But I know, if she does not, that from now on her first loyalty will be to her husband and I must take second place in her affections.

NOW MY MOTHER writes to ask why there is no word of a coronation. She asks, Is the king too poor to afford it? No one has said it, but I know there will be no coronation until I have proved my worth as a breeder of sons.

I cannot tell my mother this. I write back cheerfully that of course there is no shortage of funds. You should see what he spends on building work. His palaces will equal the best in France. This is not true, but I say it anyway.

I let some weeks pass and the summer comes and with it fine weather. I choose my time carefully. The evening has been happy and lively. It is the turn of James's musicians tonight and Master Taburner, flamboyant in a shirt of the deep blue of the cerulian dye, for he refuses to wear the red and yellow livery of the others, is playing lively variations of folk tunes. James leads me out in a pavane to start the dancing but I soon have to sit down. I can feel the drag in my belly that signifies the start of my monthly in another day or two. I resolve to wait no longer. This cannot go on.

Soon there is a cry for the faster Scottish dancing and this has become wild as usual. James joins in and collapses breathless and laughing in his chair beside me.

Perhaps stirred by the dancing, when he comes to my bed he is vigorous and playful. I hesitate to change his mood, but I can delay no longer. I must speak.

'James, there is a pilgrimage I would like to make.'

'Would you? Of course you may. My father was a great man for pilgrimages. All the time, north, south, anywhere there was a holy place. And why not. He was a more popular king, with his pilgrimages, than I am with my justiciary courts, that's certain. Perhaps he had the right of it.' His mood is fluid. He rarely mentions his father and I stay silent in case he wants to talk now, but he stops there.

'Where would you like to go?'

'This pilgrimage would not have been one for your father, but for your mother, and she had no need.'

He tenses beside me. I go on. 'There is a saint that barren women pray to.'

'I know of it. On the island.'

'I would go there.'

'Are you barren?' The question is harsh and abrupt. The answer is one I dare not speak, I dare not say Never before. Only now.

'May I, James? Please?'

Suddenly he slaps my thigh. 'We'll go together.'

THE *LITTLE UNICORN*, built at the New Haven near Leith, is ready for her sea trials. Once the captain and crew are satisfied and the wrights have made such adjustments as are needed, James and I will sail in her to Dundee, where I am to make a royal entry and where preparations are already underway for the wedding of one of James's courtiers, which we are to attend.

James says 'Why should I not skipper her myself on the sea trials?'

103

'Is it safe?'

'Perfectly safe. My wrights are the best in the world. We will travel informally.'

'You mean no one will know?' This is something he delights in, wandering round the country unrecognised, but he has never suggested I join him.

'A pilgrimage is not the occasion for pomp.'

When we arrive without ceremony at the shipbuilder's yard the men, although they know the king, look askance at me, for I am dressed in a simple woollen gown. Perhaps they take me for a whore.

The Master Shipbuilder shows us over the vessel. This is the newest ship in the fleet, small amd fast. James intends to use her for journeys north and west where speed is important. There are cabins below for us. The carving of the oak in the cabins is beautifully done and I stroke my hand with pleasure over dolphins and mermaids.

'The carver is a Frenchman, Your Grace. Master Manson.'

'Why, James,' I say, 'we must have Master Manson do more work for us.'

'He already is. He has begun carving the roundels for the ceilings in the new palace at Stirling.'

I am delighted to find that the captain who is to conduct the sea trials is Captain Wood of the *Mary Willoughby*. His eyebrows are grown so bushy I wonder that he can see. We greet each other as old friends.

The crew of eight quickly pulls us out into the bay with their oars. Then they hoist the sails and Captain Wood takes the wheel for the first part of the journey. I don't want to go below. I want to stay on deck and see everything that happens. James makes sure I am wedged comfortably on cushions in a corner at the stern and I settle back to watch.

We leave the harbour behind us and head out into the open sea, the land falling away on both sides to become only a line of blue embracing arms. The water slaps against the side of the ship and I feel the fine mist of spray on my face. As the helmsman passes the wheel over to James, the ship heels over. They ignore me as I gasp in horror and cling to the rope which surrounds the deck, but then James turns us into the wind and we are upright again. James reaches out a hand to steady me and now he laughs at my fear. Captain Wood is nodding, obviously pleased.. The ship is performing well.

James is yelping with delight at the speed and my spirits soar too, for I see the boy he must have been before the death of his father set too much responsibility onto his young shoulders.

The air smells of the sea, sharp and salty. I lean back and watch the gulls which are following the boat, twisting and turning with their raucous cries. I listen to the murmur of James and the men discussing the performance of the boat.

He gives me warning that we are about to jibe. He eases the wheel round and I cling tightly to the rope as the boat spins and with a crack the sails swing over and are filled by the wind. Another signal and another turn and we are back on our original course, heading for the open sea.

Then we settle seriously to the purpose of our journey. The crewmen set the sails and we skim over the water, startling resting seabirds who rise from the waves with angry squawks. Far out beyond the bow three dolphins leap from the water with a graceful arc and cut through the waves and out of sight again.

I can feel my cheeks glowing with the wind and spray. I pull off the damp coif and shake my hair free, revelling in the warmth of the sun on my head. The deck is steady now under my feet and I cautiously move closer to James. He loops one arm over the wheel and slips the other round my waist. The crewmen respectfully face forward, but I catch one of them winking at the others and Captain Wood has a grin on his face.

'What's to stop us sailing away?' says James. 'On and on to wherever the wind takes us?'

'And give up your kingdom?'

'Aye, to be free. By God, the lowest one of my subjects has more freedom than I have. The sea, Mary, the sea has no boundaries, no walls.'

We pass Anstruther near the mouth of the river. Faintly on the wind comes the sound of hammering, for there is shipbuilding there as well as at Leith. James points out the slips where they are building new warships. 'It is important for a modern nation to have a navy. We must protect the merchants from pirates. Too many of our vessels are being waylaid and seized.'

'But that is how you acquired the *Mary Willoughby*,' I say, remembering what I had been told.

'She was the spoils of war, captured when she was sent to prey on our merchants. I cannot depend on Henry always to be so obliging. My father began building up the navy, but he was wrong in the way he did it. He spent all the money on one large vessel, the

106

biggest ship ever built. As a boy I was taken on her once. The *Great Michael*. She was magnificent. But she cost too much money, needed too many men, too many guns. There was no money left for another great ship. But she was beautiful.'

'What happened to her?'

'After my father's death the Regent Albany sold her to the French. I was too young to have a say. Albany was more French than Scottish. Whether he demanded a fair price I do not know. I do not know what use they made of it.' He scowls briefly. 'A large number of small fast ships. That is best.'

The heads of seals bob in the water alongside us as we approach the island. At a nod from James the men drop the sails, and we drift in to the harbour. There are no other vessels there. The men toss ropes to the black-robed monk waiting and the vessel is made secure.

'Often pilgrims stop here on their way to St Andrews, but I have given orders that none are to land while we are here.'

So we are not quite two ordinary pilgrims, though we dress in simple clothes.

James pauses for a word with Captain Wood. They are to continue out to the open sea and go on testing the performance of the boat.

'There is a tradition,' says James to me. 'That you must carry a pebble and place it on the cairn. This gives a permanent reminder to the saint that you have been here.'

Obediently I bend down and search among the pebbles on the beach. There are many different colours but they have all been worn by the waves to egg-shapes and globes. I select a dark grey stone with whiter bands running through it, almost in the shape of a cross. We walk up the path to the cairn and I place the stone as near the top as I can reach. It balances for a moment then slides slightly downwards, finally nestling between two others. James has chosen a pebble too and places it carefully.

There is a good, well-trodden path to the priory buildings through bramble white with blossom and nettles from which clouds of brown and orange butterflies rise up and flutter round us, then settle back again when we are past. The priory stands in a clearing, two low stone buildings with roofs of bracken. James has been here before and knows the way. He leads me through an archway and we enter a garden where two monks, bare-legged, are hoeing a vegetable patch. They glance up and one of them comes towards us, releasing the loops which hold his habit clear of the ground. He dips his head in a cursory bow and turns away. No words are spoken. We follow him and he leads us towards the chapel. The other continues with his work.

By the door of the mortuary chapel there is the holy well and the monk raises the bucket to offer me a beaker of water. It is cold and clear. The chapel is dim and cool and is hardly bigger than the closet where my chamber child sleeps. The only light comes from one small window, through which I can see the white froth of the waves washing over rocks, and beyond that only the sea and sky. On the highest rock there stands the beacon which the monks light every night to warn mariners that here is the island. Travellers can both avoid the danger of it, and use it as a marker to win their way to their chosen harbour. For their service, caring for the bones of the saint, minding the safety of the living, the monks are left in peace.

There is a stone altar on which stands a simple wooden cross and two tallow candles burning low. I hand over the two wax candles which I have been carrying and the monk deftly exchanges the tallow candles for these. He watches them flare for a moment and as he fades back into the dimness the door closes softly behind him. Before the candles sits a plain reliquary which holds the bones of the blessed St Adrian. James and I kiss the reliquary and then kneel side by side.

I pray with all my heart and soul to God to send me a baby. I concentrate my whole being on this, and beside me I hear James sigh. His prayers will be as fervent as mine. After some time James rises but places a hand on my shoulder to tell me to stay.

I continue to kneel and pray. I pray to St Adrian. I pray to the Virgin Mary, who knew the joys of motherhood. I pray to St Clare in whose convent I grew up. I pray to them all to plead with God to send me the child that will justify me.

When the candles begin to gutter, I rise to my feet and ease my aching limbs. James is waiting outside in the darkness and together we presents our gifts to the monks, peaches and plums from the hothouse at Falkland. We share with the brothers a meal of unleavened bread and gull eggs with a cup of ale. It is eaten in silence, save for the scrape of spoon on bowl and outside the screech of a night owl. I wonder what David Lyndsay would make of this. There is no wealth gained here in pursuit of veneration of the saint.

109

'Are we going to sail home in the dark?' I whisper.

'No, we stay here tonight. The men will sleep in the boat. We will not be disturbed.'

The cell they give us is cramped and windowless. Two straw pallets have been put side by side and a rag mat placed beside them. In one corner a stool holds a candle and a ewer and jug of hot water. The door is closed behind us and we are alone.

James reaches for me and folds me in his arms.

'We'll give the saint a helping hand,' he murmurs. 'No ceremony tonight.' He pulls at the tapes of my bodice. There is no fumbling, he is accustomed to undressing a woman, though not me. In all our married life together, I have always been undressed by my maids, never by him.

His breathing becomes heavy as he kisses my breasts and I begin to feel an answering stir of desire. Impatiently I pull at his shirt and then we are lying on the bed and he is taking me without ceremony, roughly as a labourer would take his girl found alone in the woodland, in a way I have never known before, and my body responds with the first true joy I have known since I left my home.

CHAPTER 5

My coronation gown is velvet of a deep violet lined with white taffeta. Cloth of gold, James demanded, but I overrule this. No more of such finery. I have conformed to what is wanted of a queen as long as I felt unable to assert myself. I prefer dark colours and now my wishes prevail, for he can refuse me nothing.

My baby will be born in May. Before that, for there is no reason to wait, I will have my coronation in February.

After we return to Falkland from St Adrian's Isle I become briefly thinner and the women watching me wonder, for in the early days the mother's strength goes into the making of a baby and I know even before I miss my monthly course that I am pregnant.

I think I will die from happiness. When I write to my mother to tell her the glad news, James adds a postscript in his own hand. This delights Lady Antoinette so much she writes back teasingly and they exchange light-hearted letters. Any reserve my mother might have felt has been dissolved by the joy of the impending birth.

I see a new James. I see a loving man. He, who already has so many children, takes a special delight in this one.

Now the embroiderers are hard at work and extra skilled people have been called in to help with the long train, which is to be decorated with gold and silver thread, in patterns of thistles and lilies intertwined, row upon row of them. This train will be carried by ladies from the noble families of Scotland. I defy Sir David Lyndsay to mock.

There has not been the coronation of a queen in Scotland for nearly forty years. Sir David, who will be responsible for organising the whole event, has searched out the old records of the coronation of James's mother.

Queen Margaret was crowned on her wedding day, for she had the right as she was of royal blood, the daughter of a king.

I have earned my coronation. I have proved myself worthy.

'A new crown,' says James. 'Made of Scottish gold and Scottish pearls.'

The gold miners whom my mother sent last year have gone home, for the Scottish winter has proved too severe for them, but before they left they mined large quantities of gold in the hills of Crawfurdmuir. Now this gold has been given to the king's goldsmith John Mossman, to be made into a new crown for me and to gild a new silver sceptre. James's coronation gift to me is a belt of gold with a large sapphire in the buckle, to be worn over my coronation gown.

Marie tells me, laughing at the vanity of men, that Cardinal Beaton has ordered new crimson robes with matching slippers of red damask embroidered with gold thread. James himself has ordered many sets of new clothes and new tilting armour for the jousting which will fill the days of rejoicing afterwards.

THE CORONATION will be in February but first of all we rest from the preparations in order to celebrate the Christmas season at Linlithgow.

There is extra pleasure in this visit, for the work on the west wing of the palace has been finally finished and as we ride into the inner court we are greeted by the sight of the great fountain. It stands the height of three men and is topped by a sun face bearing a crown and under it, my own arms. Sparkling water pours from the mouth of the sun face and tumbles into basins and over unicorns and gryphons and I can almost imagine the stone lions shaking their manes and roaring with delight under the sparkling waterfall.

'It is not just ornamental,' says James proudly. 'The water goes to be used in the kitchens.' James Hamilton of Finnart has made this palace the finest in Scotland and as handsome and comfortable as any I know in France. When he comes to present the final accounting for the work to James, he is rewarded with the vast lands of Avandale.

We are a happy court. My consort of viols has been rehearsing the latest music from Italy. M. Columbell affects to despise the king's musicians and the competition is fierce as they take turn about to entertain us. There is laughter and singing and no longer do I feel isolated within a little French enclave.

The palace is even more crowded than usual, for many of the lords have brought their wives to see the growing belly of the queen, though as yet there is little obvious change. I could tell them that little will show until the very end, but it is beneath the dignity of a queen to discuss such matters.

It seems that the whole world rejoices.

113

The weather is cold and clear and the king rides out most days with his gentlemen. They return weary and exhilarated. The ladies skate on the frozen loch – I have learned to say loch and not lac. The doctor will not allow me to skate, though I protest that I am strong and a baby is not so easily dislodged. There is sledging on the hill. I try it for the first time, but I am too big and clumsy, so I soon leave it to the others and laugh at them when they take a spill.

In the evenings there is music and poetry and Interludes where the younger people boisterously re-enact traditional folk tales, and on Christmas Eve at my request an Interlude showing the birth of the baby Jesus. Even the candles in their sconces seem to grow quiet and still and reverent.

'A song,' cries James, and he signals for his lute to be brought. He strums softly and begins to play. With a nod in my direction he begins the melody.

I cannot be the only person in the hall this night to be thinking of the baby in my womb, the baby that augurs so well for the future. I feel a deep contentment as the lilt of the beloved French carol is taken up and we all sing softly.

Il est né, le divin enfant
Jouez hautbois, resonnez musettes
Il est né, le divin enfant
Chantons tous nos avènements.

James adds his voice, whisperingly at first then as the voices swell in harmony he sings more loudly. His voice is harsh and cracked when he tries for the top notes.

'No, no, Jamie,' comes a voice from the back. 'No more.' Everyone begins to shout no, no, and the spell is broken. He laughs but continues to sing. He persists to the end of the song and the hall erupts in applause. He hands his lute back to the usher and as the first notes of the dance music begin he leads one of my ladies onto the floor.

I turn to David Lyndsay. 'You taught him the lute? It is a pity you did not teach him to sing.'

'As well teach a corncrake to be a nightingale.' Sir David is studying me. 'Allow an old man to compliment you, my dear. You have the look of a well-contented woman.'

'Yes. I am very happy.'

He gestures round the hall. 'It is not France, but it is very fine. I would not blame you, were you to yearn sometimes for your homeland. I grew to love France, you know, when I was there but I was glad to return finally to Scotland.'

'The cardinal too loves France. You have that in common.'

His brow darkens and he glances across to where the cardinal is talking to some of the older courtiers. As he gestures the rings on his fingers catch the glow of the candles and flash brightly.

'I have little else in common with the cardinal.'

Cardinal Beaton will be leaving the court tomorrow. His uncle has died and he has been named Archbishop of St Andrews in his place. He can hardly wait to take up his duties. There will be still more wealth, more power, accruing to him with this appointment, for as primate of all Scotland he will have complete control of the Church. He will move his household into the castle at St Andrews.

'No, no,' says James. 'You cannot leave us yet. The obsequies for the archbishop will keep. He goes nowhere. Stay. Davie Lyndsay has some entertainment for us tomorrow you will particularly enjoy.'

The cardinal bows and murmurs that it would give him pleasure to hear Sir David's work. I have to turn away to hide a smile for we all know that is not true.

'Besides,' adds James, 'Gavin Dunbar is coming tomorrow. I know you will wish to converse with your colleague. You do not have much occasion to meet.'

But this makes the cardinal more insistent and James, perhaps not wanting to spoil the happy mood, gives way graciously and allows him to leave. Although the ongoing dispute between Beaton and Dunbar is whether or not the See of Glasgow should be subservient to St Andrews (for the Pope has said it is not), the mutual personal dislike of each man for the other does more to cause dissension than this. There are always quarrels, I am told, when the two men meet, so they take care to avoid one another. When they do chance to meet, they are civil in public. They would not dare quarrel openly in the presence of James.

Archbishop Dunbar is not a man to be liked. He is harsh in his judgments and brutal in his speech. There is nothing of the gentle pastor about him. Cardinal Beaton for all his wealth and display has more humanity. He at least strives to make himself liked.

James all week has been in close conversation with Sir David Lyndsay, who has the look of a man harassed. He has begun to disappear into his own quarters for most of the day. He is writing a new Interlude, to be performed on the last day of the festivities.

'It will be something to look forward to,' says James.

'What is the subject?'

He will not tell me.

On the last night I am content to watch the dancing though I am becoming uneasily aware of a tension in James. There is a flush in his cheeks and he leans forward occasionally and looks round the hall. It is as if he is counting, looking to see who is here and who is not. The hall is particularly crowded on this, Twelfth Night, for tomorrow the court will disperse and any courtier who has felt up till now that he has neglected to speak to the king, or flirt with a lady, or negotiate with one of his fellows for the sale of some land, or the purchase of a horse, will not have another chance for some time.

And then James leans back with a sigh that is as near contentment as I have ever heard from him.

'The musicians are in good form, are they not?'

'Indeed,' I answer. 'As talented as ever played for the King of France.'

'Does the King of France have as fine a poet as we have in David Lyndsay?'

The King of France does, but I do not say so. 'The tongues are different,' is what I do say. 'Words that sing in one language, sound harsh in another.'

The music ends, the sweating dancers leave the floor and call for wine. At a signal from the king the ushers call for silence.

David Lyndsay steps into the middle of the hall and whether from happy anticipation or because the tension which I sense in James has communicated itself to everyone else, the whole court falls silent and waits.

'Good people,' cries Sir David, 'I give you an Interlude.' There is a smattering of anticipatory applause.

'I give you.' He pauses. 'Reformation.'

Beside me one of my maids-in-waiting giggles nervously. I steal a glance at James. He is sitting back in his chair and now his face wears its customary closed, brooding look.

'You are not to be deaved with my poor recitation, but tonight something special. Tonight a band of travelling players has come to the palace and begged to be employed. Could I refuse? Could I, who am but a scribbler of verse say nay, King James prefers my doggerel to your fine classical art? Though poetry such as mine, I would remind you, good friends, was performed in Greece at the time of Homer, in Rome at the time of the Caesars, in Byzantium . . .'

The young bucks have recovered their nerve. There are cries of 'Get on with it, Lyndsay'.

'They have done me the great honour to ask me to read the introduction, in case they cannot make themselves heard over this rabble of uncouth groundlings. My friends, I give you A Satire.'

The ushers pull back the curtains which cover the doors at the far end of the hall and to a great fanfare of trumpets there enters the first actor, dressed

118

all in black, wearing a crown. This is a sober king indeed. He strides to the canopied throne set apart for him.

Tumbling after him come three elaborately dressed player courtiers.

One simpers his way round the hall. 'I am Placebo. I will please you. Anything you desire, sweet people.' He winds himself round the feet of the player king. Then another, who announces himself as Pit-thanke, reward seeker. He drapes himself over the back of the king's throne.

'The greatest king of all,' cries a third as he enters and bows deeply to the king. 'Flattery at your service, your most beautiful eminent grace.'

There is another stirring among the watching court and near me I hear someone, I cannot see who, murmur something that sounds like *Touché*, Lyndsay. The beginning is uneasily unlike Lyndsay's usual entertainments.

The player king heaves a huge sigh. He is going to be bored, says his expression. By my side James is chuckling softly.

Behind the player king there enters a lord, a young swaggering courtier, wearing gleaming crimson and green silks, and over them a silver breastplate. He carries a wooden sword, such as children practise with. He bows to the player king and takes his seat, the end one of three set in a row. He gazes over the heads of the audience as if the whole matter were beneath his dignity.

There is a pause and we all look expectantly at the open door, and now there stands framed in it a bishop, but what a bishop! He enters slowly, inclining his head to left and right. His cloak of gold tinsel trails on the floor, his mitre is larger than ever a real mitre is. The tip of it flops about as he moves his head and sets the long ribbons fluttering. The crozier he carries is taller than himself and glitters with glass jewels. He barely looks at the player king, merely waves a hand in his direction to an outburst of laughter from the audience. He takes his seat with great dignity.

We now know what we are to expect and sure enough there scurries in the third member of the Three Estates, for these players represent the parliament. The fat burgess bows to the player king, then to his fellows and sits down. His hand strokes his elaborate gold chain of office, a satisfied smile on his face.

'Your Grace,' cries David Lyndsay. 'The Estates are assembled.' The player king signals his wish that they should begin.

A herald calls, 'Let the petitioner come forward.'

The petitioner is a Poor Man dressed in rags. He rampages up and down the hall moaning and wringing his hands.

'My friend,' cries David Lyndsay. 'Come and speak to the parliament here assembled and state your complaint.'

'What good would that do? What good, I ask. I have lost everything and me and my bairns have to beg throughout the land for our bread. I have taken my case to the Court of Session, which claims to dispense justice to all, and to the Church courts, and got no satisfaction and since I know nobody that is close to the king, how do I obtain justice in this land?'

'State your case here,' calls out the burgess. 'Come on man. We will hear you.'

'Listen,' says the Poor Man. 'Time was when I bided with my wife and bairns and my auld mother and father on our wee bit land. We had a mare that fetched and carried and gave us a foal every year and we had three fat cows and we were happy. Then my father, who was more than four score years died, and the laird took the mare as his fee for the lease. And the vicar came and took one of the cows for mortuary fees. And then my poor old mother, grieving, followed her man to the grave within days and the vicar took another cow. And then my wife from sorrow died and the vicar took the third cow. Aye and my wife's best gown for grave-rent.'

'And did the priest himself not come to your aid?'

'Nay. When I asked him for justice he threatened me that if I did not pay his teind he would withhold the sacraments from me and my bairns.'

'Shame.' The cry comes from somewhere in the midst of the listening court. But many there are nodding their heads.

At that the player bishop stands up and signals for silence.

'It is the law,' he says, and sits down again.

There is a groan round the hall. And mutterings. Perhaps some of this audience have been poor, like the Poor Man, but they have never, so far as I know, been starving.

'I took the matter to the king's court of justice,' I understand the man to say. 'And they would hear it, but with their *avizandums* and postponements and

121

requests for further and better particulars and delays for recess and *sine die* and *pro tems*, it was two years before I had an answer and then they said it was the law and the cows had died in the meantime anyway. So here I am a Poor Man and starving and who is to listen to me?'

He rummages through his rags and finds a coin which he holds up. 'See here, I have one English groat left. And the lawyer will have that ere the day is done.'

At this a catch I glimpse of Gavin Dunbar's expression. He is sitting stony-faced. It is not clear what will happen in the remainder of the play but clearly he is already beginning to feel uncomfortable. This entertainment will not be complimentary to the Church.

He turns to James as if to expostulate and ask that the play be stopped, but James is now smiling. He is clearly enjoying the action. Archbishop Dunbar stirs in his seat as if he would rise and leave, but then obviously thinks better of it and becomes still.

'Did David Lyndsay write all this?' I whisper to James.

'Clever, is it not?'

The laughter has died and all wait to see what the Three Estates will say in the matter. Everyone here knows the truth of what the Poor Man says. They also know that the actor bishop was right. It is the law.

The Poor Man begins to rant at the excesses of the Church, at their wealth and their greed, at their concubines and the bordellos which go by the name of convents. The man speaks too quickly for me to follow it all and his accent is broad, but James by my side is quietly summarising for me.

Then the Poor Man approaches the actor king, who draws in his feet and scowls at him. He harangues him. What kind of king would allow this to happen to the men who are his subjects? Where would he be without the loyalty of the common man, who is ever ready to take up arms and lay down his life for the king in war, who works every day of the year to stay alive, only to have what little he has taken from him by the Church? The whole audience is quiet now, intent. Lyndsay's actors are speaking aloud what many think but out of caution and expediency never say.

Then the actor burgess leaps to his feet and says that it is a disgrace that the poor should be thus treated. He proposes that the Estates should pass a law. All Church lands are to be given to the poor, who will farm them. In return the poor will stand ready to take up arms to defend Scotland, should the king call for them.

The lord is nodding in agreement and leaps to his feet. Yes, the Estates will pass such a law. The bishop, angry now, says he will never agree. Why should he? It is only Church lands that are spoken of, not the lord's great estates, nor the burgess's town house or warehouse or ships.

'Ah,' says the lord, 'but you are one and we are two. And the king will agree with us.'

But the Poor Man has no qualms about addressing the bishop directly. He can speak up for himself, he says.

'I rest my case on the Bible.'

'Oh I have never read the Bible,' says the bishop and there is a roar of laughter from the spectating courtiers, but it is uneasy laughter. 'And you should not either.'

The Poor Man looks at David Lyndsay, who steps once more into the action. He is holding a Bible and offers it to the bishop.

'What?' he says, 'do you not read it? Did you never read it? Was it not strapped to your back on the day you were consecrated bishop?'

The room has quietened again. All know of David Lyndsay's opinions and all know that he can hold them as long as James allows. Since the Poor Man cannot be expected to read, it is Lyndsay who opens the book.

He turns to the actor king, bows and begins to read, translating the Latin as he goes.

A bishop must be above reproach. He must have only one wife. He must be sober, temperate, courteous, hospitable and a good teacher. He must not be given to drink or brawling, must avoid quarrels and be not avaricious. He must manage his household and control his children, for if he cannot do that, how can he control the flock entrusted to his care? There must be no scandal attaching to him.

Seated beside James, Archbishop Dunbar seems to have folded in on himself. He crosses his arms and gazes up at the furthest ceiling corner of the hall. I wonder whether Cardinal Beaton, were he here, would have sat so silently. I think he would have laughed the whole thing off as a joke.

The actor bishop is shrugging and making faces.

'Those are the words of St Paul,' says Lyndsay.

124

'St Paul, St Paul! It would be better if we had never heard of St Paul.'

'Did Jesus have property?' asks the Poor Man.

'Of course he had,' says the actor bishop, 'he was King of Jerusalem.'

He is now on his feet, stamping up and down. He proclaims that all that has been said is nonsense. He has never been married but has only had concubines. His sons are well provided for with Church livings and his daughters with good marriages. What is wrong with that? He seats himself again, satisfied he has made his case.

Now the lord is annoyed. He complains that the bishops are pushing up the price of land by buying it as dowry for their daughters. How can other people compete? Are his daughters to go unmarried because the Church has all the wealth?

The burgess joins in and they agree that the Church must be deprived of its revenues. His particular complaint is that too much of the wealth of the kingdom is flowing outwards to Rome and why should this be?

Together they turn to the actor king and recommend to him that he pass a law restricting the powers of the Church. A churchman must only have one benefice, he must earn his wages, he must preach.

The bishop is on his feet again, spluttering. Preach? Preach? Wherefore would he have time to preach?

And now David Lyndsay is addressing James, ignoring the player king, and the whole audience falls silent. He tells James that a good king should care for the whole common weal and not just for a few, that he should not favour the Church above others, that all people within the realm should have his protection as all contribute to the wellbeing of the realm.

In the silence that follows this the player king, whom nobody is looking at, leaps to his feet, and announces that he agrees with all the proposals. He walks out, with Placebo, Pit-thanke and Flattery scurrying after him accompanied by hasty ragged notes of the trumpet.

There is a uneasy movement in the audience, who are unsure whether the play is finished or not.

James startles everybody by suddenly leaping to his feet. He strides into the centre of the hall and looks round.

'You.' He points to one of the bishops. 'You.' He points to another. His hand sweeps over the Archbishop of Glasgow but none doubt that he and all the other churchmen in the room are included.

'Tak tent. Tak tent. Else I will send the proudest of you to my Uncle Henry in England and he will deal with you as he has dealt with your brethren there.'

There is a deathly stillness in the room. This is not in jest.

He turns and strides out of the hall. No one else moves. I rise, smooth down the skirt of my gown and follow him. Behind me I hear the hubbub break out.

James has not gone far, only to the audience chamber beyond the lobby, which is empty. He stops and turns when he hears my steps.

'Lassie, lassie,' he says and suddenly gives a whoop of laughter. He seizes my hands and dances me in a little jig. 'Did you see their faces. Man, man.'

'James,' I am laughing now too, 'how much of a hand did you have in that?'

The servants have left trays of sweetmeats and wine and now he pours some for himself.

'Balance, it is all a question of balance'.

'Aren't you angry with David Lyndsay? The things he said to you?'

'No, no. He has been saying the same thing since I was a child. And it does the Church no harm to be reminded that I am here and the Pope is a long way away.'

It is not fitting that the Church should be mocked at the very heart of the court, but I say nothing.

'We'd best go back,' he says. 'It would be a pity to break up the evening's entertainment so soon.'

And holding out his arm so that I may place my hand on his elbow, we go back to the hall, where silence falls as we enter. We pass through the ranks of nervous courtiers and resume our seats. The players have gone. James signals for music, the viol player draws his bow across the strings and the tension breaks.

Sir Thomas Bellenden is standing watching the dancing when James sends a page over to him and Sir Thomas makes his way round the hall to us.

'Tom,' says James. 'You thought it a fine play, no doubt.'

'Easily up to Lyndsay's standard.'

'I thought so too. I expect if Davie thought you were interested he would supply you with notes to remind you of any parts of it you have forgotten.'

The two men look at each other, Sir Thomas smiles, bows and backs away.

'Good, good,' murmurs James.

CHAPTER 6

At last February comes and it is time for my coronation. We move to Holyrood Palace.

Edinburgh is *en fête*. James, wishing to consult his master gunner about the coronation salute, dons the old clothes he wears for travelling incognito among the people and makes his way on foot up to the castle. He comes back in exuberant mood. Every building is almost hidden under flags and banners. The streets are being swept and reswept and echo to the sound of Highland and Lowland tongues, from north and south, east and west, for everyone wants to be here for such an occasion, not seen before in the lifetime of many. Ambassadors from every country are here and the burgesses are determined to show off Edinburgh as the finest city in the world.

From Holyrood Abbey comes the constant sound of hammering as the carpenters build the scaffolding needed to seat all the people. All the nobility of Scotland have been sent letters summoning them to attend, as if, says James, we could keep them away.

He slides a hand round my waist. 'Not all of them are happy,' he says. 'This bairn confounds many an ambition.'

I keep quietly to my own apartments as much as possible. The baby is due in three months and already I can feel him kicking. The physicians make me rest, so I have little to do but sit in my room and stitch cradle clothes with my ladies, who are clearly aching to be out enjoying the excitement of the preparations.

'This will not do,' I say. It is a fine, clear day and all traces of frost have gone. We will walk slowly to the nearby village of Canongate, where Queen Margaret has taken lodgings.

James knows I occasionally visit her there. I am ready to argue with him if he expresses disapproval but he gives no sign of his feelings one way or the other. His new benign mood almost embraces his mother.

She is fatter than ever and there are tendrils of grey hair drifting out from under the coif she wears in the house. She is attended these days by only one lady. Perhaps few wish to be associated with her in case they incur the wrath of the king. Lady Catherine is a thin, silent presence in the background. She is a poor relative of Margaret's second husband, the Earl of Angus. When I first found this out I said to James that it was a pity his mother had so few ladies and the one who serves her is of a family who are James's enemies.

He shrugged. 'I cannot exile them all. Besides, when my mother sends messages to her brother in England she uses that spindly shank of a lady and I know about it. If she had too many servants round her I could not keep track of them all.'

Queen Margaret seems to me to have lost the vigour which was evident at my wedding. She is brooding on the past.

'As you grow old,' she says, 'all your life becomes vivid to you. You relive it again and again.

130

Keeps you awake at night. You are haunted both by the past and by death, which waits nearby.'

'Pray God not for a long time,' I say dutifully, but in fact the Dowager Queen is ageing quickly.

She hardly hears me. 'I hope you will never find yourself in the position I was in,' she continues. 'A widow with a child that is a king and all the lords waiting to seize power if they can. Half the nobility of Scotland have a claim to the throne. I know they blame me for marrying so soon after my husband's death, but what can a woman do? I needed a strong man. It is not my fault that when my son reached manhood Angus did not want to let go of his power.'

My visit to the Dowager Queen has not lightened my spirits.

JAMES'S USHER comes with a message. All my household are to attend a mass to be held in the abbey the next day and if I am well enough I am to be there also. He gives no explanation for this unusual request. Since we came to Holyrood Maître Guillet has served mass to me quietly in my own private chapel. Besides, the scaffolding in the abbey is not complete and the carpenters will not be happy to stop.

The abbey is full. As well as my own household, most of the king's gentlemen are here and many of the visiting lords and their wives. Every churchman in Edinburgh seems to be in attendance, the cardinal, Archbishop Dunbar of Glasgow, the Bishop of Ross, several others, all in their full canonical robes. Black friars and white friars stand in groups. Even Maître Guillet has been pressed into service. The mass is served with full ceremony. The incense seems stronger, the singing clearer and more fervid, as well it might be, for the abbey choir contains the finest voices to be found in Scotland and is larger than usual in preparation for the coronation mass.

Unusually, Cardinal Beaton himself preaches. It is a lengthy sermon and in French.

As I lead the way out of the abbey I meet Sir David Lyndsay and Sir John Borthwick waiting at the door. Their presence is surprising. Neither is known to be a devout attender at the mass. They are with a tall blond man in an excessively padded doublet and sleeves slashed elaborately to reveal the snowy shirt underneath.

David bows deeply and presents the stranger: Sir Ralph Sadler, ambassador newly come from England. Now I understand. We have all been pressed into service to demonstrate that Scotland is a true daughter of the Church. I wonder whose idea it was. James's or the cardinal's? I can only hope that the earnest churchmen taking part in the display have no inkling that its purpose was less than spiritual.

I say the right things. The ambassador is most welcome. I am glad there is peace and amity between our two nations. By two nations of course I mean Scotland and England, but as we are speaking in French perhaps Sir Ralph can choose to take it I mean France also. Peace, I reflect as he graciously returns my compliments, might be possible but amity is unlikely.

I return to my quarters. I know what is expected of me. I change my simple gown for one that is more elaborate and send for the jewel casket. Soon the summons comes. I am requested to join the king in the long gallery.

Sir Ralph is there too.

'I have asked Sir Ralph to convey to King Henry my uncle our pleasure in the news of his new marriage. I am sure he and the Lady Anne of Cleves will be well suited.'

'Indeed,' I agree. 'Please do assure King Henry of our personal pleasure.'

Sir Ralph bows. None of us believes a word of this. Cleves is a Protestant German state and Henry's marriage will push him further away from Rome than ever. On the other hand, there are already rumours that Henry is not happy with this new wife, his fourth.

'I wish the king and his wife a long and happy marriage,' I say.

'And a fruitful one,' says James.

Sir Ralph is carefully not looking at my belly.

'Observe, my dear,' says James and he gestures to the courtyard below. Six geldings are being put through their paces.

'A gift from my uncle,' says James. 'Are they not very fine?'

'Very,' I agree, though I think we already have better in our stables. 'The king is most generous.' There is a subdued glee about James, but the reception of an ambassador is a serious matter.

'The whole world knows that England breeds fine horses,' I say.

'It is true, ' says James. 'They achieve a good mix with blood from overseas.'

Sir Ralph bows at the compliment, but he must know that it has come to our ears that the English people are calling Henry's new wife the Flanders Mare, whether because of her appearance or because of her

133

unequivocal role as the best hope for King Henry's desperate search for more sons.

'May I crave an indulgence?' asks Sir Ralph. 'I believe the gracious lady the Queen Dowager is at court. I wonder if I would have your permission to visit her, to convey to her the love of her brother.'

'You do not need my permission.'

As we watch Sadler leave James says, speaking softly so that he may not be overheard, 'the king my uncle does not part with the best of his horseflesh, even to his favourite nephew. No matter. I have asked the Bishop of Ross to give up his house as a lodging for Sir Ralph. I would be sure that Sir Ralph understands that we and the Church are in perfect agreement with one another.'

'It is said he is in total sympathy with the new learning, not just to please his king.'

'That is why I have asked Davie Lyndsay and John Borthwick to look after him. They will have much to talk about. They all read the same books.'

'Heretical books.'

'Perhaps. I would have Sir Ralph know that I do not need to crush dissent in my kingdom in order to rule.'

He takes my arm to escort me back to my own apartments. 'Sir Ralph reports to Master Cromwell, who looks for any opportunity to persuade me to follow my uncle's example and take the Scottish Church away from Rome. It is amusing, is it not, to make sure that he sends bewildering and contradictory messages back to his master?'

At the evening banquet Sir Ralph is seated between Cardinal Beaton and Archbishop Dunbar. On this day they have set aside their differences and are in accord with one another. Whenever I look over, both are talking at once to the ambassador. John Borthwick on the other side of the hall raises his glass to Sir Ralph as if in sympathy and Sir Ralph raises his glass in acknowledgment. James has seen the exchange too. He winks at me. I try to keep my face serious as I turn back to Lord Maxwell, who is telling me an interminable tale of how he cleared Liddesdale of murderers and cattle thieves.

IT HAPPENS that I am with Queen Margaret when the English ambassador is announced. Lady Catherine produces from somewhere an old-fashioned English gable hood and fits it carefully onto her mistress's head. She brushes some crumbs off Margaret's front and then hastens out to tell the boy that Sir Ralph may be shown in.

'Sir Ralph, I hope you have comfortable lodgings.' He assures her he has.

'I would have welcomed you to my own house,' she goes on, as if she has not heard him, 'but unfortunately I do not have a house of my own in Edinburgh. My funds do not allow it. I am kept in penury. The allowance I was promised by my brother Henry has not arrived this quarter.'

I indicate that I will go and leave them to discuss their business in private, but Queen Margaret shushes me. 'Stay, please,' she says. 'Sir Ralph, what message have you brought for me from my brother Henry?'

'He is in good health and hopes that you are likewise.'

'I am not, as you can see.'

'He is concerned for your well-being and asks that I determine you are well cared for and all is well with you.'

'Concerned? So concerned that he cannot be bothered to write a letter to his sister! I have not heard from him for some time. Henry did not need to send an envoy. It is clear from the absence of any communication these many months that he gives little thought to me. Perhaps he is so poor with shuffling on and off wives that he cannot afford a little piece of paper and some ink to write to his sister and find out how she is. I am clearly forgotten in England, but Sir Ralph, I will not forget England. Perhaps if it were known here that I had not been forgotten by England I might be better thought of.'

I am sure these are things not meant for my ears and I rise. Queen Margaret turns to me and commands me to stay. Sir Ralph has leapt to his feet and for a moment I detect a sudden plea in his glance at me. Perhaps he thinks that left alone with the Dowager Queen he will hear even worse. I subside back into my seat.

'Is Your Grace ill-treated?' asks Sir Ralph bluntly, sitting down again.

'I am not ill-treated. I am ignored.' She shouts this last word and it leads to a fit of coughing. Lady Catherine hastily gives her a glass of wine. The coughing stops and the anger appears to dissipate. She holds out her hand to me.

'I am well cared for since this dear lady came to court. We are good friends, are we not?'

I agree.

136

She turns back to the ambassador. 'Is the Prince Edward my nephew in good health?'

'In the best of health, Your Grace. He is now near two and a half years old and thriving.'

This last is not what we have been hearing from our agents in London. The word is that the child is small for his age. What Queen Margaret hears from her own agents I do not know, but she replies sharply.

'Pleased to hear it, sir. Because if anything should befall him, the bairn in this lassie's belly, my grandson, might yet be King of England.'

CHAPTER 7

I tell James of the scene in his mother's house. I feel some unease that speculation on the succession to the throne of England should be so aggressively thrust into the notice of the ambassador. It can only cause ill-feeling. It is something we do not speak of. Indeed I can almost forget that James is half a Tudor, so much does he seem to dislike them.

'How did Sir Ralph react?'

'He ignored it. We went on to talk of other things and I left as soon as I could. She should not have spoken as she did. King Henry has a son living and is surely not too old to sire another. And there are the two daughters.'

'If Henry is to be believed, both of doubtful legitimacy. Besides, England would not thole a female ruler. No, my dear, Henry's throne could yet pass to me and mine. Why do you think he hates me so much? But the Queen Dowager should keep such thoughts to herself. The sooner she returns to Perth the better.'

This conversation disturbs me, I am grieved to think that anyone should speculate about the death of the baby Prince Edward, or about any child.

THE HALL is lively tonight. James's musicians, in tribute to Sir Ralph, play some English airs while we dine, some composed by King Henry himself. Then because the ambassadors from France and Spain are also present they make way for my musicians, who know the latest music from those countries.

Sir Ralph readily answers the questions my ladies put to him about the latest fashions in London. Skirts, he tells them, are wider than ever, and petticoats more embroidered. The sumptuary laws are being broken all the time. 'No merchant's wife can bear that she cannot dress as the ladies of the court do, for there is no money wanting in the city and what better way for a man to show off his wealth than in the jewels and clothes of his lady.'

'Such vanity in women is not confined to London,' murmurs David Lyndsay. There are protests from my ladies and calls from the gentlemen to repeat his amusing, to them, poem, but he only smiles and shakes his head.

After the meal the court settle to their amusements. I have determined that I will not gamble so much, so I do not join the card game. In an alcove the page boys are throwing dice. The younger people sort themselves into sets for a slow strathspey. I notice Maître Guillet deep in conversation with two of the king's chaplains, seemingly undisturbed by the noise around them. Now might be the opportunity to talk to him, to find out what seems to be making him unhappy.

When his companions have moved away I catch his eye and signal to him to join me.

'Are you happy here in Scotland?' I ask.

'Yes, Your Grace. It is a great privilege to serve you.'

This is not what I am asking. 'You perhaps miss your home?'

'My home is here now.'

'Do you find the companionship of the King's chaplains congenial?'

'They are all learned men.'

'But have you become friends?' This is a question too far and I see he is struggling to answer me.

In the early days he seemed eager to open himself up to me and talk about all manner of things, for we were both finding it all new and interesting, but now he has closed up and I hesitate to force his confidence, which may not be willingly given. I leave the matter there for the present.

Meantime Sir Ralph has eagerly acquiesced in James's suggestion of a game of chess. The chess set is brought. It is the board of gold and silver with the chessmen of jasper and ivory. The only time I have seen this before was when James took me round the treasure house. It is not the one with which he plays regularly.

They are evenly matched. The game is a long time playing out. In the end it is Sir Ralph who tips his king over, acknowledging defeat to murmurs of appreciation from the watching courtiers.

James rises and invites Sir Ralph to join him in his private quarters and signals to me to come also. Once there he calls for wine and then dismisses the servants. I indicate that the heat is too much for me and seat myself a little distance away with a glass of watered wine and some candied fruits. I pick up my sewing and compose myself to be the invisible woman forgotten in the background. James wants me here because tomorrow he will ask me to recall what is said.

He will ask me what my sense of the conversation was. When Sir Ralph said this or that, did he mean this or that, or something totally different? Are there matters on which he turned the conversation, matters that he did not wish raised? At the same time my presence must not inhibit the talk, for men, even diplomats, will talk more freely if they forget the presence of a woman. I am better than a spy behind the arras.

Sir Ralph leaves off the polite conversation and turns to the matters he is here to discuss.

'His Majesty has asked me to raise with you the possibility that the two of you might meet to discuss matters pertaining to both your realms.'

'As my mother's brother he is dear to us,' says James. 'I have always felt sad that with so much in common we have never met.'

'I understand there have been other occasions planned but not fulfilled.'

'Ah, yes. The first time, some eight years ago, all was arranged, but I caught the smallpox. On the other occasion I had actually set sail, but contrary winds drove the fleet back and by the time the weather was kind once more the moment had passed. Kings, Sir Ralph, are at the mercy of the elements no less than their subjects.'

Sir Ralph is clearly in no mood for philosophical debate. 'Can such a meeting now be held? This year?'

'You know,' says James. 'It could be made even greater if King François could also be present. Three kings together, who knows what might be agreed. Another crusade perhaps. It is the dream of every red-blooded king to lead a crusade, is it not?'

I can almost read Sir Ralph's mind as James is speaking. Whatever Henry has in mind it is not another glorious encounter with François. It is said that the last meeting, known as the Field of Cloth of Gold, nearly bankrupted the English exchequer. And kings might talk of a crusade, but none of them wants to initiate one. Sir Ralph cannot tell if James is serious or not.

'I will convey your thoughts to His Majesty.'

'I would welcome my uncle to Scotland at any time.' This of course is not true. No English king has set foot in Scotland since King Edward was defeated and no amount of diplomacy could smooth the path for such a visit.

'He was hoping that you would visit him at Hampton Court.'

'Alas, I could not spare the time to journey so far south. I am not so willing as Henry to leave the government of my kingdom to others.'

This is a dig at Master Cromwell, who is said to rule England, as Cardinal Wolsey did before him.

'I observe that Your Grace's council seem to be very young.'

'Their fathers died at Flodden, as mine did.'

Sir Ralph deems it expedient at this point to excuse himself to the privy.

'Do you feel well enough to stay?' asks James. I do.

'We'll loosen his tongue.'

When Sir Ralph returns James offers him a change from the wine they have been drinking.

'You must taste this,' says James. 'This is made especially for me. I think you will like it.'

James pours him a generous glass of *uisge beatha*. He does not offer it to me as it is not a drink for women. It is harsh and makes the head spin. James describes how the drink is distilled from grain specially for him, as for his father, at a monastery near St Andrews. It appears something similar is made in England from juniper berries. The talk becomes trivial. They talk of hunting. Sir Ralph boasts of how King Henry spends long days in the saddle. Mention of Henry brings the talk back.

'A meeting?' asks Sir Ralph.

'An excellent idea,' agrees James.

'King Henry has in mind to visit the northern parts of his kingdom.'

James sighs, 'Yes, indeed. No doubt the realm is more peaceful again. I hope the late rebellion has not left a mark. Bad business.'

'It was nothing,' says Sir Ralph. 'Labourers, unhappy with their lot.'

James is not so discourteous as to disagree with him.

Sir Ralph heaves himself more upright in his chair and persists. 'When His Majesty comes north? A meeting?' I catch James's eye. Sir Ralph is becoming intoxicated.

'Perhaps.'

The two men fall silent. Sir Ralph sips his drink. It is clearly to his taste.

'Your Grace,' he says. 'I would touch on a most confidential matter.'

'Go on.'

'Unfortunately,' he pauses. 'It concerns some correspondence between your Cardinal Beaton and his

144

agent in Rome. A letter from the cardinal was most regrettably delayed on its way.'

'How did this happen?'

'The messenger was taken ill. He was well looked after but it seems less care was taken with the letters he carried. They were rescued by one of King Henry's men and in order to protect them from further harm, in deference to the source of them, he passed them to His Majesty.'

'And did King Henry read this confidential correspondence?'

Sir Ralph bows his head in regret and does not answer.

'In Scotland,' says James. 'We regard private correspondence as . . . private.'

'Alas. It was inadvertent. You know what it is like, I am sure, so many missives cross the desk of a king. The contents are absorbed before one realises what they are. The clerk who had opened the letters was of course reprimanded.'

'And did King Henry then send them on to where they were intended?'

'Of course. With his most gracious apologies.'

'No harm done then.'

'In the letter,' says Sir Ralph, 'the cardinal expressed unease about Your Grace's intentions towards the Church.'

'The cardinal is not privy to my intentions towards the Church.'

'Perhaps Your Grace considers that the Church in Scotland needs reform, as it did in England.'

'I govern my kingdom, the cardinal looks after Church matters. Each in his sphere. I see no need to interfere.'

'There is great wealth in the Church. His Majesty understood that such wealth being sent to the Bishop of Rome would be better kept within England, for the greater good. Perhaps the cardinal is concerned that Your Grace should think likewise.'

'Perhaps the Church in Scotland is more generous. I have only to ask and it is given to me. The Holy Father has consented on many occasions that I may levy a tax on the Church for good purposes. The Church, for instance, pays for the maintenance of our Court of Session, where justice is dispensed. No, Sir Ralph, I thank you for drawing the matter to my attention. I will myself convey to the cardinal that he has no cause for worry. It has been a momentary misunderstanding perhaps.'

James stretches his legs out and leans back in his chair. I insert another stitch in gold thread into the baby gown. The shutters creak softly and the flames flutter in the grate, though we are sheltered on this side of the palace from the wind which sweeps down from the crags. James, I have observed, has had less of the *uisge beatha* than Sir Ralph. Considerably less.

Sir Ralph plunges on. 'Rome was displeased when you ordered the release of some heretics.'

'They are good men. Why would I want them burned?'

'Why do you tolerate heretics, but dislike the idea of reform of the Church?'

'I do not dislike men who think for themselves.'

146

This is said softly, gently. It is known that King Henry is becoming intolerant of any man who disagrees with him. None of his closest advisers can count himself safe if he opposes the royal will.

'Why,' James continues in the same quiet voice, 'why should I seek to make myself head of the Church, when the Church already does everything I ask of it?'

'His Majesty hopes that after you allowed the play that was performed at Linlithgow you might be moving towards his way of thinking.'

'Henry knows of our little Interlude? I hope I do not have spies within my court reporting to foreign sovereigns.'

'Such talent as your Depute Lord Lyon's poetry is famed abroad.'

'We are proud of him.'

James is leaning back in his chair with his eyes closed. Sir Ralph is slumped, gazing into his glass. He raises it and looks through it at the fire. He sighs.

'There is the matter of the sheep.'

When he says this I almost laugh aloud. Not the sheep again! Henry would try and control everything James does, but the sheep in particular have become an obsession with him. James maintains that it is because England's wealth is built on wool and Henry fears competition. He would prefer that Scotland remain poor.

'Sheep?' James does not open his eyes.

'His Majesty considers it beneath the dignity of a king to keep sheep.'

'I keep sheep. On my estates in Eskdale.'

'Quite . . . quite so.'

'The sheep,' says James, 'is a most useful animal. It gives both wool and milk and finally meat. I hope my Uncle Henry does not despise the sheep.'

'It is a lowly occupation. In the opinion of King Henry.'

'Lowly,' repeats James. He opens his eyes and reaches out to fill Sir Ralph's glass. 'Can anything a king does be considered lowly? Is a king not above such judgments?'

Sir Ralph clearly has his orders and he holds tenaciously to the purpose.

'His Majesty suggests you leave such occupations in the hands of your subjects. The dignity of one king reflects on the dignity of all. So says His Majesty.'

James does not answer him and the conversation dies along with the fire. James rises and indicates that the evening is at an end. The ambassador's man is waiting to see him back to his lodging. We take a gracious leave of him, with the promise that the next time Sir Ralph travels to London he must take with him a bottle of the royal *uisge beatha* as a gift to King Henry, and one for himself.

When the door has closed behind him James murmurs, 'So Henry would sow discord between me and the cardinal, would he?'

As I wrap up my sewing in its silk sheath I ask how King Henry knew so much about the Interlude at Linlithgow.

'Tom Bellenden writes regularly to the English warden of the eastern marches, who reports direct to Thomas Cromwell.'

'You allow that?'

148

'Of course. If I want Master Cromwell to know something, Tom Bellenden obliges.'

He offers me his arm to escort me to my room. 'The survival of a crown may depend on a network of informers and intelligencers.'

And I, I think contentedly, am the closest and best of them all.

IT IS DONE. The crown is placed on my head, the mass is served and I am *La Reine d'Écossais*, the Queen of Scots.

There is a moment of farce before the ceremony when a page comes rushing in to say that the cardinal cannot find his breviary. It has likely been years since he used it, I hear someone mutter. Fortunately Maître Guillet, who has been by my side in all the preparations, has his and lends it to the cardinal. It gives me extra happiness to know that a breviary from my homeland is being used in my coronation here. As I kneel to receive the host I smile at the cardinal's new crimson and gold slippers peeping out from under his robe.

The glorious voices of the choristers of the king's chapel choir send the new music by Master Carver soaring towards heaven. I find myself almost weeping with relief as I bow my head in gratitude to God for the child in my belly.

I wish my mother and father could be here. My grandmother would be more than ever convinced of God's destiny for me. She might tut at the expense and have a quiet smile at the opulence of the cardinal, but she would be secretly glad.

JAMES WANTS the baby to be born at St Andrews where the palace is being made ready for my lying-in. As soon as the coronation celebrations are ended we travel across the River Forth.

James himself was not the last Scottish royal baby to be born, twenty-nine years ago, but his younger brother, the last of Queen Margaret's children, died. Now he insists everything must be new and fashionable. Master Manson has already arrived to build the new royal cradle. He has been busy carving the ceiling roundels for the new palace at Stirling but these, he tells me, are nearly done. His sketches for the cradle are delightful. I remind him of the first time I saw his work, in the great cabin of the *Little Unicorn*. I will never forget that happy journey with James.

Now I have nothing to do save rest and walk in the garden and stitch clothes for the baby. It is the springtime and the air is full of hope. Crops are being sown, and every day the fishing boats come in laden with heavy catches. Even the trading vessels queueing in the bay to use the busy harbour seem to flaunt their colours with more joy.

Queen Margaret, taking advantage of the king's new benign mood, has followed us and taken lodgings in St Andrews. When he learns of her arrival James just shrugs. He seems not to mind too much that she comes every evening to hall to dine, telling anyone who will listen that she does not eat so well at home for the king keeps her short of funds. They are civil in public and take care not to meet in private.

'It's a first grandchild. It is important to a woman,' I say to him apologetically, though why I should be apologising I do not know. It is not, of course, a first grandchild: there are all the bastards. I do not know whether she has acknowledged them. They are too young to be seen at court, but the day will come soon when James will want them near him. Arrangements are already being made for little Jane Stewart to enter my household. The boys are destined for the Church. I can foresee the day when the influential churchmen round James will be his own sons. But my son will have precedence.

Queen Margaret comes to my chamber practically every day to sit by the fire and talk to me. It is as if she has been walled up in solitary confinement and has had nobody to talk to. Lady Catherine sits with my ladies but has nothing to say to them. Occasionally I see her shaking her head at the frivolous talk of the younger women. Her expression says, as you see me now, one day you will become. They eye her warily and occasionally fall silent under her cold gaze.

Sometimes I dismiss all the women and Queen Margaret and I are alone. We are two queens with one destiny, the bearing of an heir for Scotland's throne, though she never quite forgets that she is royal born and I am not.

'I had seven and they all died, except for James and my daughter to Angus.

'James is a good king.'

'In his way, but he will never be the man his father was.'

I am shocked and have no reply to this. I put the words down to the idealisation of a long-dead husband that one often finds in sad, lonely old women.

She goes on. 'My husband was a saint. The people loved him. They don't love James, for all his going among them and playing the peasant.'

James has more immediate things to worry about. There is unrest in the Western Islands of Scotland. Ever eager for travel, for movement, for activity, he himself will lead a pacifying force. He sends orders for ships to muster at Dumbarton.

'These chieftains who call themselves lords of the isles must learn there is only one lord, one king in Scotland.'

'Surely you will not go till after the birth of the baby.'

'I can go and be back before then.'

James leaves for the west, but he has only been gone a day when the pains start. 'It cannot be,' I tell my women firmly. 'It is something I ate.'

I am wrong. The baby arrives early, on the 22nd of May, and comes easily, a healthy boy.

The messenger who is sent to Dumbarton to tell James he is the father of a fine new prince is in time to catch him before he embarks and soon he is striding into my room, still in his travelling clothes. His attention is immediately on the baby. He strokes the tiny hand as if he had never seen one such before.

'Every king of Scotland for five generations has been James and so will this one be.' Three of his bastard sons are called James, but clearly there is room for another. He calls his clerk and dictates a letter to his Uncle Henry to advise him of the birth.

I send word to my mother and father and now there is a flurry of clerks as letters are written to all the sovereigns of Europe. Letters of congratulation pour in, including one from my uncle the Cardinal of Lorraine, who assures me I have no kinsman more eager to do me service. He is sending James a gift of three Spanish horses.

James is in such good humour that when he accidentally meets his mother in my chamber, he speaks kind words to her. She heaves herself to her feet and congratulates him on the birth. He thanks her and wishes her good health. And then since they have nothing more to say to one another, she leaves us. Neither of them smiled.

I am weepy from the birth, which has brought back memories of the births of my other two sons, my François, now growing up in France without me, and the little baby Louis, who was taken from me by God. I pray and pray that this little one will live a long and healthy life.

THE DAY OF his baptism comes. I cannot be present: it is not the custom and I am not yet churched. The cathedral is prepared and the churchmen have gathered. From my window I see the crowds milling round, lords and their ladies, the burgesses, the townspeople.

'So many?' I say to James. 'Come for the baptism of our son?'

'Partly. Partly for another reason.'

'What reason?'

'One that will please you. The trial of a heretic.'

Yes. Heretics must be stamped out. There have been a number of such trials lately, for since David Beaton was raised to the office of Archbishop of St Andrews he wields unrestrained power. The

153

punishment is brutal, death by burning, but most of those tried are allowed to recant, are fined and that is an end of it.

'Who is to be tried?'

'John Borthwick.'

'Borthwick? Our John Borthwick?'

'The same. Banned books have been found in his house. Luther, Melanchthon, others.'

'But you knew that. You have always known that. You said so when you assigned him to look after Sir Ralph Sadler.'

'This is Beaton's doing. He must make an example.'

'You are allowing it? Sir John is your friend. A good man, you said. One of your faithful servants.'

'All that.'

'Then why?'

'It keeps the cardinal happy. Don't distress yourself. It is not good for your recovery.'

'You would burn an old friend and a good servant? You are no better than your Uncle Henry.' I am screaming at him in my distress. I cannot understand what is happening. I lift my fists and hit him on the chest. He seizes my hands.

'Calm yourself. There will be no burning. John Borthwick has already taken ship to England, where he will be welcomed with open arms. He is safe there. Or as safe,' he adds, 'as any man can be in Henry's England.'

I sink back in my chair, weeping uncontrollably. Irritated, James paces the room, occasionally looking out of the window at the towers

154

of the cathedral, standing clear against the pale eastern sky.

'When is this to happen?'

'It has already started.' And it is true. The precincts of the cathedral have grown quiet, as most of the people have gone inside.

'The cardinal will be a happy man. The Pope will be happy. And generous.'

'How could you allow this, James? On the day of our son's baptism?'

'Beaton will have time for both.'

James does not want to be seen to have anything to do with the trial and goes off hunting with Oliver Sinclair and some others of his gentlemen. If they understand what is in James's mind it is more than I do. Occasionally from the cathedral comes the roar of the crowd, as something is said that meets with their approval, or not. I puzzle over the whole business. I climb back into bed and fall into a doze. I am still tired from the birth and sore.

I dream of my first husband, Louis, and the baby in France who died. I dream they are both being dragged to the stake while I scrabble at the faggots round their feet but the flames rise higher and I can do nothing to save them. I wake up sobbing, to the smell of burning. Marie has her arms round me, shaking me.

'It is only straw. They have made an effigy and are burning it. It is the only burning that will happen.'

Our son is baptised. The godfathers are the cardinal himself and the Earl of Arran. Whether this honour is enough to gratify him, now that with the birth of this boy he is displaced from his position as heir to the throne, no one can say. In his congratulations on the birth he has been courtesy itself.

Queen Margaret is one of the godmothers, Marie another.

'I have never seen a man so glowing with joy as the cardinal,' Marie tells me afterwards. 'He was almost floating off the ground in his happiness. No one knows how Sir John Borthwick was warned. He slipped away safely, but the cardinal is happy because he was found guilty and it is a splendid example to everyone. How could the king be so deluded in his servants as to allow such a man near him?'

The baby begins to grizzle and I pass him to little Jane Stewart to hold for a moment. She is now one of my maids-in-waiting, a quiet watchful child. Already she worships the baby and hovers over him every hour she can. He is passed to the wet nurse, who bares her breast and the child sucks greedily. The pain I feel is more than a physical ache. The midwife has prepared a dish of herbed ale to drink to reduce my milk, but the needs of my baby will be met by other women and not by me. He will have his own household, as befits a prince. He is no longer mine. He belongs to Scotland.

The day after the baptism James returns to the western expedition. He will sail on the flagship the *Mary Willoughby*. Also sailing are the *Salamander* and the *Little Unicorn*. I send my compliments to Captain Wood. They will be accompanied by a large fleet of ships, more than sixteen great vessels carrying the king's household and the troops – several thousand of them – and provisions for all of them. Sir Robert Maxwell is in command. Lords Arran and Huntly have mustered their men and Cardinal Beaton is going, with a large number of fighting men from the Church estates.

I am uneasy when I hear of the extent of these preparations. James assures me there is no danger. He does not anticipate any fighting. This is not what I am told by the women as they sew and talk. The men he is taking with him are all his friends, all young, all lively, all out for adventure. Who can say what might ensue when the blood is up and reputations are to be won?

It is the burden women bear, my mother writes. To wait at home while the men go to war. She knows what she is talking about. How often in their life together has my father ridden off to join his king on the battlefield? But always, praise be to God, he has returned. I can only pray that James will return to me unharmed.

Meantime I spend as much time as I can in the nursery. The baby thrives and I soon recover my health. James has had a comfortable litter made for me, with brass ornaments and hangings decorated with thistles and fleur-de-lys and lined with fat velvet cushions. It is designed to be carried by four sturdy little mules in the care of the muleteer I brought with me from France.

'We will be as comfortable as may be in this, Antoine,' I say cheerfully to him and he mutters something under his breath which I do not catch but think it wise to ignore, for he considers everything in Scotland inferior to France. I am carried around the town, along the river and up onto the cliffs where I can breathe in the clean fresh sea air, watch the restless waves and dream of James's return.

He is away almost a month. When the news comes that the fleet is safely back in Dumbarton harbour I order a mass to be sung in the cathedral to give thanks for this. There was very little fighting and a great deal of talking with the clan chiefs. James has brought back a number of hostages to enforce the loyalty of the island lords.

With his return it is time for the court to move to Stirling. I must leave my baby behind. I will have my duties as queen to perform, and there should be no time and no place in my life for the baby. He will have his own household here in St Andrews.

When I go to the nursery to say farewell to him and the nurses, I find James already there. He is standing beside the cradle with one hand on the top of it. I wait for a moment in the doorway. He has not heard me coming. His mouth is turned down and the fingers resting on the top of the cradle are tap, tapping.

As I move quietly forward I hear him sigh. He says, 'When a king has a son there is a rival for his throne. The boy is a threat to him from the day he is born.'

'This is a fine boy who will grow up loyal and brave. And when the time comes he will make a fine king, for you will have taught him how.'

'But when that happens I will be dead.'

AT STIRLING CASTLE James leads me up onto the wall walk where we can look over the new palace which is being built in the-south west courtyard where the old buildings have been demolished. The new building is almost complete, the outer walls painted in the King's Gold, while the statues in their niches glow brightly with fresh paint. There are craftsmen at work decorating the rooms.

On our other side the carse stretches away before us. James names to me as he always does the distant mountains, while far below the river winds through the rigs bright green with the growing grain. A raven circles above us, calling out in his harsh voice. I want to pull off my hood and let the wind blow through my hair, but I have to refrain for the inner court is crowded with people carrying in our gear. Until the new palace is finished we will live in the old palace, built by James's father.

'If ever,' he says, 'there is danger, this is the safest of all the castles. Remember that.'

'Why should there be danger?'

He shakes his head and does not answer me.

All is not well with James. A new air of anxiety hangs about him. Because he is always on display, as I am, in the crowded court, he keeps his face impassive, but sometimes in private the mask slips and I catch a glimpse of something like despair. He is never angry. He seems subdued, but his fingers go tap, tap and I wait for an explosion of temper which never comes.

He grows thin. He is white-faced and drawn and there are large shadows under his eyes. When I express concern he turns his back and walks away from me.

He used to spend hours of every day with the clerks, the treasurer, the almoner. He has always worked hard. Now, despite the constant stream of messengers backwards and forwards from Edinburgh, from St Andrews, from Glasgow, from Aberdeen, from overseas, he seems unable to concentrate. Privy council meetings are brief and nothing is decided. Justice ayres are held without him, ambassadors spend their time in courteous amusement with me and my ladies and wait for a summons which does not come.

I question his physicians but they say they can find no physical cause for this, except that he eats but little, as if food has lost its savour. I press them and hesitantly they suggest that the humours are out of balance, but he will not allow any to treat him.

I question the chamber child who shares the king's bedroom. The boy tells me that the king does not sleep well. Frequently in the night he rises and wanders round his suite of rooms and often he will open the shutters and stand for hours gazing out, sighing. When the child asks if he needs anything, ale or herbs for pain, the king does not even hear him. He sometimes summons his dressers while it is still night and they have to dress him by candlelight. He shuts himself up in his library but when the clerks arrive in the morning there are no letters drafted, no plans made.

He comes to my chamber often, but he does not want love. It seems he only wants not to be alone. He lies awake staring at the ceiling as the moonbeams chase one another across it. I try to pleasure him, to stir him into some emotion other than this empty coldness, but he draws away. He throws back the bedclothes and rises, to wrap himself in his fur gown and sit by the embers of the dying fire.

He has taken to prowling round the new palace, examining in detail the work that has been done since the last time we were here. He talks to the carpenters and masons and he continually studies the drawings that Hamilton of Finnart has had done.

Sometimes I come across him standing looking at a new wall, or at the sculptors and painters perched under the ceiling on their scaffolding. He used to do this in a happier mood and take visitors round, drawing attention to the French-style glazing in the windows and the ceiling bosses showing all the chivalric arms of Scotland. Now, he just stands and gazes without a word and makes the men nervous so that they mis-hit their chisels or drip paint, and if it is the precious blue or gold they freeze and wait for an onslaught of anger, but James says nothing.

'My lord.' I take his arm and lead him gently down into the garden where we pace round and round and I talk about little things while he walks silently by my side. I draw his attention to the plum trees which I ordered from France and which are now thriving, and the roses, which are blooming though the gardeners shook their heads and said they would not do. Occasionally he will stir himself and give a brief answer but he does not look at me. I feel a chill which has nothing to do with the weather, and take his arm while I prattle inanely about the letters from my little son François, who has become obsessed with horses and wants the king to send him some Scottish stallions.

'Yes,' he answers. 'Yes.'

But nothing interests him. I go into his room one day and find him gazing moodily at a new book on his desk.

'What is the book?'

He does not answer, just pushes it towards me. It is fresh from the printers and smells of leather and ink. It is a new volume of the translation of Boece's History of Scotland, which James has ordered to be translated from the original Latin into Scots.

'It is a beautiful book. You haven't cut the pages yet. Shall I do it for you?'

'As you like.' He turns away and I put the book back on his table.

I have troubles too. Money is becoming a problem. There are so many people to be fed and housed, so much expenditure on clothes and jewels. A letter has come from my mother to tell me that Chateaudun has lost the salt concession and this will reduce my income. This is not the first such letter.

In the past I have taken such letters to James for his advice. But I see now I cannot. I tuck the letter away to answer later. The solution must be in my own hands. This is not the time.

THESE DAYS the court is very quiet as the lords, one after another, observing the king's demeanour, slip away, pleading business elsewhere. It is only on special occasions this is a grand crowded court in the manner of King François, for the gentlemen here all have estates and business of their own to look after, while many have been delegated by James to maintain justice and peace in their own country. None is idle in the way of the French lords. But now there are even fewer people here. One man who lingers is the Earl of Arran and sometimes I catch him eyeing the king with a speculative expression on his face.

Even Oliver Sinclair is nervous. In the evenings James no longer plays cards or chess, which he always loved to do. He has never while I have known him been one of those kings who must win at all costs and whose courtiers only play with him out of courtesy. James wins or loses with equally good grace. Indeed I sometimes wondered if he likes to lose and toss over the coin as much as to say, there is plenty more where that came from.

Now he does not play but sits at the head of the hall watching his courtiers at their nervous amusement. I tell the musicians to play folk tunes which James has loved in happier times. So many of the songs are melancholy and tell of long-ago battles or lost love and the courtiers silently listen and sometimes there are tears in the eyes of my ladies and even one or two of the men. If I can but bring out the melancholy that is poisoning him, in the way a wise woman will use a herb that looks like the illness of her patient in order to cure him, he will be himself again. He does not react. He just sits there and his fingers go tap, tap, tap.

It is as if he hears nothing but his own thoughts.

SIR RALPH SADLER, pale and agitated, comes to ask leave to return to London. His master – not King Henry but his other master, Thomas Cromwell – has been arrested and charged with treason. James is grave and sorrowful and gives Sir Ralph leave to go, but does not release him until he has given him some words of advice to pass to King Henry.

'Henry should learn from me. It is a mistake to allow one man in a kingdom to grow so powerful. First Wolsey and then Cromwell. My uncle allows himself to be ruled. And they betray him in the end.'

Cardinal Beaton is elated. 'The man is punished for what he did to the Church in England.'

'God punishes in the end,' I say.

'Aye, of course.'

Cromwell is executed, by the axe, perhaps the same axe and the same axeman that ended the lives of those saintly men More and Fisher. 'So the devil may have his own back,' says the cardinal. 'And welcome to him.'

There is amusement in the court when word comes from England that King Henry has declared his marriage to the Lady Anne of Cleves annulled and has married another of the Howard clan, a little girl younger even than the Princess Mary. They say his son the Prince Edward is sickly, and he must try to get another quickly. When such talk is brought to me, I hush it. No one but God can give good health and God can take away a healthy child as quickly as a sickly child.

These thoughts are in my mind when I receive a message from St Andrews. One of the nursery maids has been sent to tell me the baby is ill.

In my anxiety I go running to James, who questions the messenger. The baby has been vomiting. 'The wet nurse?' I ask. 'Is the wet nurse ill? Is there disease?'

'Her milk dried up. They found another.' The girl is shifting uncomfortably.

'Why was I not consulted?'

The girl is blushing. She did not expect the king to be present while we talk of intimate matters.

'I will go to him,' I say.

'No.'

164

Quickly I bundle the girl and her escort out of the room.

'Please James. I know about babies. I can make sure everything is done.'

'No.' He is shouting. 'Your place is here with me.'

I dare not argue. But next day even as I am scheming to find a way of going to my baby, word comes that the vomiting has stopped and he is well again. It was only the change of milk. I wonder though, if the people in St Andrews are telling the truth. Do they make light of the problem for fear of the king's wrath? Have they heard rumours that he is ill and do not want to worry him?

One of my ladies is to return to France, for she has word that there is illness in her family and she wishes to be with them. Joanne's people are our neighbours at Bar-le-Duc, my father's estate.

My mother scolds me for being a poor correspondent, but does not understand how busy I am. Besides, I must be careful that matters of state do not find their way into my letters. A careless word can be misconstrued. Letters can go astray. So when I write I confine myself to innocuous family matters, or matters concerning the management of my estate in France.

Now I have something I most surely cannot confide in a letter. I can trust Joanne. I commiserate with her over the illness of her family when I give her letters to carry. She is taking many such letters from others in my household for their families. But for the one matter I cannot put in writing she is to seek a private interview with my mother.

I swear Joanne to secrecy but I know she has never been inclined to gossip with the Scotswomen of the court. My confidence will be safe with her and to make doubly sure I tell her she is released from my service and will not return to Scotland.

'Say to the Lady Antoinette I worry that the king suffers from melancholia. Ask her what I can do about it. Ask her to send me some medicines. No one must know. And no one save my mother must know that I worry about him.'

Several weeks pass and then one day a Scottish priest just returned from France is brought to me with a letter from my mother and some phials containing physic. I reward him well and send him to Maître Guillet. There are letters for him too, from his family.

I show the medicine to the king's physician. He sniffs the phials and holds them up to the light. Some are familiar to him, some are not and he is intrigued. But still he shakes his head.

'I dare not,' he says. 'His Grace is terrified of poison.' He adds, 'As might be any monarch.'

I leave off trying to persuade him. He is afraid, too. He does not know what these preparations are. If any cause the king harm, it is the doctor who will be blamed and suffer for it. I dare not administer anything myself to James.

And so I watch my husband deepen further into his misery and can do nothing to help him.

IT IS EARLY MORNING and Oliver Sinclair is talking to a woman in the far corner of the garden. I do not immediately recognise her, but as she turns and for a moment looks towards the palace I see who she is.

They will not be able to see me among the trees. I draw back and call softly to the dogs so that they stay with me and do not disturb the couple, who in any event are intent on their conversation.

'Run in and fetch me a cloak,' I tell little Jane Stewart who is my only companion today and she obligingly hurries off.

This leaves me free to watch the couple as they stand, their heads together. I know her now. She is Lord Erskine's daughter.

I have seen her only once before, at the inauguration of her nine-year-old son, the cleverest of the Stewart bastards, they say, as prior of St Andrews. James was not there. He avoids such events. That all of his sons will be provided with lucrative posts within the Church is a matter for the Church and not for him. So the proprieties are observed.

But on that occasion, with James absent on one of his brief circuits to his estates in the south, I had positioned myself so that I could see the boy, his mother and stepfather as they entered the cathedral.

Now, I can see that the two years which have passed since then have not been kind to her. She is thin and as she bows her head to listen to whatever poison Sinclair is pouring into her ear I can see that her shoulders are slightly hunched, as if she is developing the stoop of middle age. She is older than I by several years. As I watch they move away towards the palace.

Later Oliver Sinclair approaches me. 'A gift for the baby prince.' I weigh the beautifully wrought whistle in my hand. It is small but heavy, of good-quality silver. He asks for the latest news of the prince and I tell him the boy is teething. I want to ask if the gift is from himself or from someone else.

'Was that the daughter of Lord Erskine I saw you with in the garden today?'

He is momentarily discomposed but recovers quickly. 'Yes, we met by chance. She had come to visit her father. I have not seen her for some time.'

'You know her well?'

'Years ago, before her marriage took her from the court.'

'And has she now returned to Lochleven?'

'I do not know. I would suppose so. She said nothing about going on somewhere else.' The answer is too full. Smooth though he is, I think to myself, you are lying.

An usher comes to tell me they are ready for me in the Presence Chamber. Today is the day I hear petitioners.

There are many supplicants today. As well as the usual matters, pleas for alms for elderly relatives or a place for a younger son or daughter in my household, now the demands are greater. Many who would in the past have approached the king now hesitate and deem it expedient to channel their petitions through me. The room is crowded.

I scan the waiting crowd. There is no sign of Margaret Erskine. Nor of Sinclair.

When I have dealt with as many of the petitioners as courtesy requires, I signal to George Seton, who is acting as gentleman usher today, that there will be no more. Before there can be any ceremony, while those nearest me are hastily rising to their feet, I have left the chamber.

I push aside Oliver Sinclair, who is lounging outside the king's door. He protests loudly but I am already in the privy chamber. They are alone. She is kneeling by his chair and holding his hand. They look up as I enter and I see defiance in her face, but his has the closed, frozen look that has become familiar to me these last few weeks.

'Lady Margaret,' I say, 'when I saw you in the garden earlier I was expecting you to join us in the hall.'

She has risen to her feet. 'Your Grace is kind. But I have lost the habit of company.'

'I think the king is tired now. Perhaps before you begin your journey home you will join me in my room for some refreshments?'

She dare not refuse and James says nothing.

I order sweetmeats and wine and once these are brought, dismiss the servants. Lady Margaret is calm, her hand steady as she raises the cup to her lips. We sit in the window seat and look out onto the gardens. She remarks on the new tennis court. I comment on the fruit trees, brought from France. She compliments me on the winter colour.

I ask after the health of her husband and of her son. She has several sons but we both know the one I mean. I do all this calmly. What is past is past. I am not such a fool as to be jealous of a discarded mistress. Discarded, I remind myself, for all her presence here today.

There is a pause.

'Your Grace,' she says, 'I came here today because I heard the king was ill.'

'A passing cold, nothing more.'

169

'There is a melancholy about him.'

'Briefly perhaps. Overwork. It has worn off. He is himself again.'

We both know that she saw today that James is not well, that the rumours are true. Why, I wonder, do I not admit this? She has known him for far longer than I. If this woman was so close to James, perhaps she and I could be, if not friends, then at least not enemies.

But it is no use. I do not want to talk about my husband's illness. I have nothing to say to her.

But then as she rises to go she looks down at me, still seated, her face crumples as if she would weep and she spits out, 'you should never have married him.'

'I had no choice,' I cry.

'It is me he loves. He always has.'

'Love has nothing to do with the marriage of kings.'

'He wanted to marry me.'

I rise and walk towards to the door. I am shaking and cannot bring myself to answer her. I, of all people, recognise tears of anger and frustration. Have I not shed enough of them myself in my time?

'He would have named our son as his heir.' She is almost screaming now. 'Marriage to you has made him ill.'

I open the door and find Oliver Sinclair there with her waiting woman. Have they heard?

Lady Margaret walks away. Sinclair makes to follow her then turns back.

'The Lady Margaret . . .' he begins.

'I do not wish to know the Lady Margaret,' I say and he steps back, bows and turns away, but I catch a smirk on his lips.

There are undercurrents here I do not understand. Is it his affection for James that makes Sinclair cleave loyally to the woman? And if that is the case, does James still wish he could have defied his advisers and married her? Is it true what she claims? Suddenly I have a vision of the two men together talking of me, comparing me to the Lady Margaret. No, I will NOT imagine such things.

In my bedchamber I dip the cloth in the scented water in the ewer and rub my face with it. I breathe deeply to compose myself and concentrate on what is in front of me, the coat of arms painted above the fireplace, the arms of all the men from who I am descended. There are the Barois dukedom and the red and gold bands of the King of Aragon, the four gold rings of Jerusalem, the double cross of Lorraine and the fleur de lys of the Dukes of Anjou. My father is a Duke of France and my uncles are dukes and cardinals.

And most reassuring of all one half of the shield shows the royal arms of Scotland, the arms I am entitled to bear because I am the Queen of Scots. I may not be of royal blood, but my line is ancient and honourable. Who is the Lady Margaret Erskine but the daughter and wife of lordlings of no account, save for what use the king can make of them? It is I who wear the crown and not she. I live in the king's palaces and she does not. These suites of rooms are mine, and it is my boy who is the prince of Scotland.

But I fume in vain and I know it. I am not the woman James wants.

Love is not a word either of us has spoken. His letter to me so long ago did not ask for love, or offer it. I know now I would give the crown and all the wealth that he has bestowed on me as his queen to hear him say that I have his love also. But I know that I must settle for second best, as he has done.

And I wonder whether it is true what she said. Is it marriage to me that has made James ill?

IN MY ORATORY Maître Guillet is standing in front of the altar. In a court which has become quiet and watchful, my household chaplain has been even quieter than usual.

He is not praying but gazing intently at the triptych behind the altar. I make to withdraw but he starts and bows. He says nothing. I move to his side and look at the painting. The Virgin has long red hair, not unlike my own. It is on the tip of my tongue to remark that my own baby prince has not such a fine head of hair as the fat little baby Jesus lolling on her lap, when I become aware that Maître Guillet is weeping.

'I have worshipped the Blessed Virgin all my life,' he says in such a low voice I can hardly make him out.

'And will go on doing so,' I say after a pause.

There is another long silence and I wait, tense. Then, 'In France I was safe.'

'I do not understand. You are safe here.'

'In France, in our quiet church, there was never any doubt. Here they question, question, question all the time. They never stop.'

'What do they question?'

172

'The Church. Her teachings.'

'Who have you been talking to?'

'Your Grace, it was unwitting. When we are in St Andrews I was permitted into the college library.'

'St Salvator's College?'

'Yes. They have a wonderful library. It was the books which attracted me in the first place.' He is twisting his fingers together as he speaks, as if he would crush them. 'Those beautiful volumes, they tempted me. I could not resist. The feel of smooth vellum and the beauty of the script, of the illustrations. Oh my lady, I felt my cup running over with happiness. And now I can never go there again.'

He began to thump his chest. '*Mea culpa. Mea culpa.*' I reach out my hand to his and grip it.

'Go on, Maître. The old books, they hold nothing that should trouble you.'

'Would that I had restricted myself to the old. But they have new books, Your Grace, new printed books. Do you know the sweet odour of a new-made book? The college houses scholars who have travelled the world. They bring back these books and worse.'

'Worse?'

'They bring back ideas. I have been drawn into talk.'

'Learning is a fine thing. How are we to learn without books and discussion?'

'Yes. But they go beyond anything that is . . . that is safe. And then, at Linlithgow, when we were celebrating the birth of the baby Jesus, I listened to Sir David talk of the cupidity of the Church and I burned with shame to think I was part of it. I tried to close my mind to what he was saying but afterwards we talked amongst ourselves. We could not help it.'

'We?'

'Some of the men about the court.'

The mischief-makers.

'Sir David was not casting doubts on our worship of the Blessed Virgin,' I say. 'He was attacking the way the Church takes money from poor people. You do not do that. There was nothing there that could disturb your peace of mind.'

'Not in that, no. But the talk of the scholars goes beyond what the Church does, whether it is greedy or not, beyond that, to whether the Church is right in all it says. They say none in the Church can point to where in the Bible it speaks of Purgatory and if there is no Purgatory then for what do the poor give their pennies to the Church? They question whether the saints, or the Blessed Virgin Mary can intercede with God. They say God does not need intercession. They say priests have no right to offer absolution. Only God can do that. And what is to stop any man appealing direct to God?'

'You should not listen to such talk.'

'I wish I had not. But I cannot put it from my mind.'

'You begin to have doubts?'

He looks round desperately. 'Your Grace, I doubt whether I have the right to absolve you from your . . . when I hear your confession. I do not know if any man has that right.'

This is the heresy that Cardinal Beaton would protect the Church from. This is the heresy that sent John Borthwick into exile. I am listening to this wicked talk in my own private oratory from my own priest.

174

'Have you spoken to anyone else about this?'

He shakes his head. Not even, it seems, to his own confessor, who would have given him absolution, something I cannot do.

'Do you wish to return to France?'

'No, I would not . . . I would not wish to leave your service, Your Grace.'

He is the only person here to whom I have been able to confide my deepest secret fears about my husband's sanity. This has been done under the seal of the confessional and with the pretence that my fears are a sin to be absolved with a penance, but we both know that the outpourings of my despair are a plea for understanding and reassurance from another human being and have little to do with God. And now I am the only person in whom he has confided his torment. Yes, I think. Torment is not too strong a word. Already I can sense an easing of his grief.

And I have become fond of him. What am I to do?

'Maître, it is my wish that you return to Chateaudun.'

CHAPTER 8

George Seton has brought Marie back to court, in full health after the birth of a son. I rejoice with her in the happiness of her marriage and her pleasure in the stepchildren who love her.

Her company is all I need. I intend to make a pilgrimage, one without ceremony and most particularly without anyone's knowledge. I tell her what is in my mind and she is taken with the adventure of it. For a brief time we are like girls again, giggling over an enterprise of which we know our parents would disapprove, but my jollity is forced.

We are at Falkland for the summer and I choose my time when James is in Edinburgh where his presence is essential, for the Three Estates are sitting and the Court of Session has numerous petitions to hear.

Marie begs some plain clothing from the wardrobe, saying that she and some of the maids-in-waiting are planning a masque about fisherfolk to amuse the king.

'I had difficulty finding something long enough for you,' she says.

The excuse I give for my absence requires some thought. I dare not say I am ill. The only person I can consult is Maître Guillet, who is still here, awaiting a ship for France.

'I know you have doubts,' I say. 'But I have none. I believe that if I make this pilgrimage my husband will recover.'

His advice is sensible. 'We could give out that you are spending the day in retreat and prayer. No one will intrude.'

We slip out of the palace in the very early morning. Marie has arranged for two mules from the stables, telling Antoine that she and a friend are going to visit an old servant of Lord Seton and do not want any fuss made. If he recognises me as I lurk by the gate waiting for the mules to be brought, he will keep his knowledge to himself. He mixes little with the grooms, who despise a mere muleteer and a French one at that.

We are clear of Falkland before the sky is properly light. The road to St Andrews is well made and broad and even at this early hour it is busy with farmers taking vegetables, meat and fowl into the town, and with other pilgrims. Most are on foot, a few riding mules or donkeys and here and there a cripple in a little cart being pulled along by his friends. I see a child carried on a makeshift litter of wattle and I avert my eyes. The pilgrims are of all stations. Many are dressed in quality clothing, plain for travelling. A few are in rags and some beg alms as they go.

Marie passes down a coin to one such and soon we are surrounded by others. We set our faces against them and ride on. I do not want to be cruel but I cannot risk being recognised. Marie hisses at them and they go away.

The spires of the town come into sight. Outside the walls we dismount. Marie takes the mules to a tavern to be put in the care of the ostler. I stand under the eaves and keep my face covered while I listen to the chatter of the inn people around me as they bustle about their business. A man speaks to me but his voice is guttural and I cannot make out what he wants. I turn my back and pull my veil more tightly over my face. Everyone else ignores me. I am just another pilgrim.

When Marie returns we settle our shawls over our heads and join the crowd. I have never entered the town before on foot, in a crowd and unrecognised. We have always entered with the royal cavalcade, with the road cleared in front of us.

We shuffle into the cathedral. We take water from the holy well beside the door and make the sign of the cross. The cathedral has a different aspect from what it has on the high days. I have often been inside since my wedding here, but always with the court and always with some ceremonial.

Now there is no red carpet and the stone slabs are cold under my feet. I hold a pomander to my nose to mask the stink of the pilgrims crowding in. Beside me a man holds out an arm towards the distant high altar and as his sleeve falls back to expose a suppurating wound the smell of it reaches me and I almost retch. In the nave there are lunatics chained to pillars. The one nearest me has soiled himself. One is screaming, shrill above the hubbub of the prayers that are being shouted or sung or just muttered by the pilgrims.

We follow the crowd, which is moving along the north ambulatory, intent on their purpose. Around me I hear many languages, Spanish and Dutch, English, and for a sudden moment I hear the familiar French, but I dare not turn my head.

At every side altar and chantry there are priests serving mass and banks of candles burn brightly, while behind them, all is in shadow. I ease myself free of the crowd and kneel at the feet of one of the statues of the Blessed Virgin. The tiles are warm under my knees, the warmth of the woman who made way for me. I drop some coins in the box and light two candles, one for my dead husband, one for my dead baby, but my prayers are for the living husband.

I rejoin the moving crowd and soon we are approaching the relic chapel. We file in and kneel before the carved sarcophagus. Within it is the casket that contains the holy bones of St Andrew himself.

Surely, surely the saint, the patron saint of Scotland, will hear my prayers. Beside me a woman is sobbing. On an impulse I reach out my hand and take hers. She gasps and quietens. When she looks down at our clasped hands and I follow her gaze I see that her hand is red and roughened with work and mine is smooth and white. She tightens her grip for a moment then unclasps her hand from mine and turns away.

The monks move us on and we shuffle round to the south aisle. Here I kneel at the feet of a statue of St Andrew and repeat my prayers.

It is enough.

At the door there is a canon selling pilgrim badges. Marie gives him a coin and takes two.

When we leave the cathedral we pass the palace where my baby son is in the care of his nurses. I long to visit him, but of course I cannot. I make a silent prayer, offering up my yearning as a gift to God.

We are back at Falkland Palace by nightfall and slip in unnoticed.

In my oratory I find Maître Guillet. He has been there all day and as I enter he rises stiffly from his knees. I am dropping with weariness and begin to weep when I see him.

'You have done everything you can, my lady,' he says. He puts his arm round me in an embrace. I lean my head on his shoulder and wish that I could sleep for ever and not wake up.

In the privacy of my bedroom I choose blue embroidery silk and stitch the pilgrim badge into the hem of the nightgown I wear when James comes to my bed.

CHAPTER 9

Sir James Hamilton of Finnart kneels in front of the king.

'What is it they say I have done?'

'You know what you have done. I saw. I saw with my own eyes. I was there.'

'Where, Your Grace? When?' This is said wildly. Finnart has been dragged from the arms of his wife before dawn and told he is under arrest. He has the desperate look of a man living through a nightmare. He is bareheaded, there is blood in his hair and his right sleeve hangs in shreds. The guards who have brought him stand impassively at the door, out of hearing save when the king is shouting, as he is now.

I do not want to be seeing this, but I have to be here. Not knowing what is happening would be worse. I wrap my fur gown more tightly round myself. I have not had time to dress but my shivering is not wholly from cold. Round us there are the subdued sounds of the palace coming to life. I sense the servants moving around quietly, heads down, wary of drawing attention to themselves.

James has not told me why he has had Finnart arrested. He has told nobody and now he will not tell Finnart either. The others in the room attracted by the noise, Oliver Sinclair, George Seton, stand by, silently. Even Arran, Finnart's half-brother, who has drawn back into the shadows, says nothing.

James nods to the guards and they come forward to pull Finnart to his feet. He shakes off their arms and straightens his shirt. He stands very straight and attempts to look James in the eye, though James will not meet his.

'I have served you faithfully, Your Grace. You know me for a true and loyal servant. Whatever poison they tell you is a lie.'

And he turns his back on James and walks from the room, the guards following. When the door opens there is not the noise from the hall that there usually is. All is silent. The uneasiness of this whole court is like a miasma rising from the marsh that is the king and his illness.

'Tell the stables to prepare.' His gentlemen hastily step out of his way as he strides from the room.

Within the hour James has ridden away, no one knows where, accompanied only by one servant. He takes no gentlemen with him and they continue to hang about the hall, looking stunned and talking in low voices. He stays away overnight and although George Seton at my request makes discreet enquiries to find out where the king slept that night, the groom who accompanied him refuses to say.

THE TRIAL is held two days later.

'I do not understand,' I say to George Seton, who seems to have aged suddenly. 'He is a friend of yours, is he not? ' He nods. 'Can you not speak to James about it? What is Finnart accused of?'

He tells me. The charge is causing a gun or other weapon to be fired when the king was present and this had happened on more than one occasion.

'I have no recollection of this. When was it?'

'Eleven years ago.'

'Eleven . . . ? And he is only now being accused?'

George Seton seems as bewildered as I am. 'The man is a good servant to the king. Most of the new building you see has been his work. He has done everything James wanted. He has created beautiful palaces for the king out of old castles. I do not understand why Jamie should turn against him.'

'Are there any other accusations?'

'That he plotted with others to enter the king's bedroom and kill him.'

'This was eleven years ago also?'

'No, this year.'

'But that's nonsense. We would all have known about it at the time.'

'Yes. But there is also a suggestion the prince's life is in danger.'

This shakes me. 'Could that be true?'

'I don't know. There is always talk of plots against kings and their families but I have no sense that such might exist here. Jamie has brought peace and the rule of law to Scotland and we are all more prosperous because of it. He has intelligencers everywhere. Maybe they have heard something.'

'What will happen to Finnart?'

'That will be for the court to decide.'

'Who will be his judges?'

He lists them. The Earl of Argyll, who is Chief Justiciar, Sir Robert Maxwell, Huntly, Somerville, Erskine, others of Finnart's peers, the Earl of Arran.

'His brother? His brother will be one of the judges at his trial?'

'His half-brother.'

'Even so.'

'There is no family feeling. Finnart has always maintained that the old earl was not married to the present earl's mother. If that were true then Finnart would be earl now. He had control of his half-brother's estates until the boy came of age. Then Arran accused Finnart of embezzlement. It has never been resolved. And Arran has resented the king's generosity to Finnart. He will not hesitate to sit in judgment on his brother.'

I shake my head in despair. The lords are all related to one another and many are related to the king and they squabble like children in the nursery. But squabbles do not lead to trials for treason.

'Cannot the cardinal intervene? They are friends, are they not? Finnart has helped in the search for heretics.'

'The cardinal has found it expedient to make a tour of the north. He will not intervene.'

'Is this the matter which has been troubling James these weeks past? Why did he not tell me, particularly if our son is in danger?'

He shifts uneasily. 'When a king mistrusts one he mistrusts all.'

'Even me?'

It takes only a day for the court to proclaim Finnart guilty. Within hours he has been taken to the Mercat Cross and publicly beheaded. It is done so quickly that even the Edinburgh crowds, who dearly love a good execution, have no time to gather.

THE COURT is quiet. Those who have no choice but to remain here are careful not to attract the king's attention. He spends many hours with the clerks and law officers. It is whispered that he is going over the papers left by Finnart and that many of them are being destroyed and certainly, although it is August there are large fires kept going in the king's quarters.

I hear James shouting and hurry into the clerks' room. The exchequer clerks are there and Oliver Sinclair. There is an open kist on the floor and a clerk is kneeling down, lifting out coin bags which he hands up to another clerk.

James picks up one of the money bags and empties it over the floor. Gold coins spill out and roll in every direction.

'Gold,' he shouts. 'How much?'

'Three thousand two hundred pounds so far,' says the clerk and goes on counting, but his hands are shaking.

'Three thousand pounds? Three thousand pounds. Gold. Hidden in his coffers. And at whose expense? Whose expense, tell me that?'

But no one dare answer him. Why should Finnart not have a store of gold coin? His estates are large and fruitful.

The king giveth and the king taketh away. All the estates, the lands, the gifts, the offices, which he gave to Finnart across the man's years of service to him are taken back and given away to others. Oliver Sinclair comes hurrying out of the king's room, looking pleased with himself.

'Gloat now,' I hear someone murmur. 'It could be you next.' I look up from the card table, for we are trying to give a semblance of normality by going about our usual evening pursuits. The speaker realises I have heard and reddens and drops his gaze.

The person who gains most from Finnart's downfall is the young Earl of Arran. He is granted new charters confirming his earldom. They describe him as a familiar counsellor of the king and are granted for special love and services both in France and Scotland. He is given extensive parts of the lands which were Finnart's.

James auctions Finnart's possessions. But not all.

He shows me a silver pyx. I have never seen one handled before save by the priest serving mass. I feel a faint qualm. James is looking at it as if it is just another box. He holds it up to the window, the better to see the detail on it.

'It will do for the prince's chapel at St Andrews.'

'Where has it come from?'

'The silversmith will engrave it with our son's arms.'

'Whose was it before?'

'It is part of the chapel graith of the late traitor. There are other pieces I've ordered to be sent to St Andrews.' He indicates a small kist at his feet. 'Candlesticks of gold, a fine enamelled incense boat. I wonder where he bought that. I would like one similar, but these meantime will go to our son.'

'No, James. Please not. It is not fitting that the chapel gear of a dead traitor should be used in our son's chapel.'

'Why not? The man is dead. Where he is now he has no further use for them. And God doesn't care who owned them before.'

I have no argument, save a feeling of distaste which I cannot put into words.

In the weeks that follow I watch Arran swaggering about the court in new-found familiarity with the king. But he is not the only one to have benefited from Finnart's downfall and I can only keep my thoughts to myself.

I WAKE to find James climbing into my bed. I put my arms round him. He is icy cold. Through the gap in the bed curtains I see his chamber child hovering, his feet bare, his face pale with anxiety. The candle he holds in his shaking hand is guttering.

'Tell me,' I whisper to the boy.

'He woke screaming and ran from the chamber.'

'Go back to bed. I will look after him.'

The child persists. 'Is he ill?'

'A bad dream,' I say.

'He has been crying in his sleep.' The whole bed is trembling with James's shuddering. But I must reassure the child.

'It's all right,' I say. 'Something he has eaten. Go back to bed and don't mention this to anyone. His Grace would be angry if people knew he was upset by some mouldy food.' I don't know if I can trust the child to keep quiet. Possibly not, but what can I do?

189

In the faint moonlight from the window I can see the gleam of James's wide, horrified eyes. I pull the quilt tightly over us. I wrap my arms round him and pressing my body close, opening my legs to embrace his. After a while the shivering stops. There is no arousal. I do not expect there to be.

The illness of my husband is beyond the power of the body to heal.

Eventually his breathing becomes easier. He starts to speak but cannot find the words. I wait, uttering the soothing nothings a mother will murmur to a baby.

'He came to me.'

'Who did?'

'Finnart. He came to me and he . . . ' He chokes and cannot go on.

I wait.

'We were fencing. But it was not in game. He cut off my arms. They were lying at my feet and blood was pouring out. He said he would come back and cut off my head. He stood and laughed at me. And there was nothing I could do for I had no arms.' This ends in a sob.

'It was but a dream.'

'Was it? Was it?'

'The moon shining in the window has disturbed your sleep.'

'Was it an omen?'

We lie awake for a long time, but towards morning he falls asleep, a heavy noisy sleep with occasional gasping sobs. I hold him in my arms, cramped, but I dare not move to disturb him. When the servants come in with hot water he stirs. For a moment

190

he looks at me as if he does not know me. Then he slips out of my bed, swishing the curtains apart and startling the girls.

I hope the court will believe the king and queen had a night of passion. If they can think that then so much the better. It will still any gossip and convince them all is well.

I believe nothing can ever be as bad as this again.

AND THEN I begin to wonder whether I am once more pregnant. My courses have been irregular with the worry of James and I cannot be sure. If there is a child, then it was not conceived in passion. James in his despair has turned to me without caresses or kisses but only as a physical relief from his misery. There have been a few such occasions and perhaps one has resulted in the child I may now be carrying.

NOTHING LASTS for ever. Those who counselled patient waiting are eventually proved right. As the trees turn from green to brown and gold James seems to recover his spirits, though he still suffers from nightmares. When he wakes in the morning he has forgotten them. I do not tell him that many nights I hold him in my arms while he moans and mutters in his sleep, a sleep I dare not disturb.

As he recovers his energy and some of his spirits we make a progress to the west, for he would have me see those parts of the realm that I have not yet seen. These are prosperous lands, with a great wide busy river and rich farmland. It is a fairly subdued court which travels, but the people welcome us everywhere and give us gifts for the baby prince.

There is the added pleasure of my pregnancy, for I am now sure I am carrying a child. The joy is more subdued than when I carried the first baby, but enough to promise hope for the future.

When I begin to suffer from vomiting I agree reluctantly to return to Falkland. We attend together a mass in the cathedral in Glasgow, where Archbishop Gavin Dunbar gives us his blessing. Then I turn reluctantly for home and leave James to carry on his progress westward and southward.

Unencumbered by me and my ladies he makes a great sweep of the south and into the far south-west, pursuing and punishing malcontents and criminals with fresh vigour, settling neighbour disputes and checking on the country's defences. Any rumours there might have been about his illness have surely died away.

This pregnancy is not as easy as the others. With increasing discomfort comes listlessness. The winter is wet and when it is not raining a cold mist rises from the sea and envelops the land. Wraiths appear and form themselves into illusory shapes and fade again. All is shifting, uncertain. I long for the dry, warm air of France, where all is clear and bright. When I wake in the morning and feel the chill in my room despite the fire which has been burning all night, I lie under the quilt with my eyes closed and daydream of sitting in the garden at Chateaudun with the warm sun on my face and the smell of lavender in my nostrils. Then the maid comes in and stirs up the fire and I have to rise.

When James returns from his travels and joins me at Falkland he seems happier. Cardinal Beaton, as if sensing that the time is propitious, returns again to his preoccupation with the heretical literature coming into the country. He brings to James a list his people have compiled of the merchants who are believed to be implicated in this trade.

'It's coming in through Dumfries and Ayr and other west coast harbours. You saw for yourself how many of them there are and how hard they are to control. They think because they are remote from here they can do as they wish. There are already deluded people there turning their backs on the Church. There are ports within sight of England and Ireland and the evangelicals slip over and contaminate our people and are gone before they can be caught.'

'Busy, active harbours, with much prosperity,' says James. 'Important for trade with France and Spain.'

'I also have reports of pamphlets circulating in Aberdeen.'

'Tell Huntly. That's his domain. Ask him to investigate and report to me, but to do nothing more yet.'

The cardinal tightens his lips and goes on. 'In Montrose a preacher has been openly using the English Bible. He fled before my men could arrest him. This filth is spreading throughout the country. I have the books burned as soon as they are found, but more keep coming in.'

I listen to this in silence. I dare not make any comment. No one has questioned why Maître Guillet has returned to France. His replacement has had to come from within the ranks of those serving James. I chose an elderly Scotsman who preaches platitudes and shrives me gently for the peccadilloes I confess to him. I keep my other thoughts to myself.

I wonder if the cardinal is aware that within the colleges in St Andrews itself they are talking in a way that might destroy the Church. Perhaps he is so busy with his ambassadorial duties to France and with the management of the rich Church estates, and advising the king and parliament on how to run the country, to notice such things.

He is still arguing with James.

'We must stop this trade. See, here is an example, James Bullock, merchant. He was found guilty before, paid his fine and now he's been caught with copies of pamphlets printed in Antwerp and Geneva. It was a mistake to be lenient before.'

James does not even hesitate. 'No,' he says. 'Leave the merchants alone.'

He issues orders that every merchant travelling to the continent has to bring back armaments on his return journey. They complain. They send a deputation from Leith to ask for some leeway. The weight, the space which hagbuts and culverins take up seriously limits the cargo they can bring back for their own profit and they are not happy about endangering their ships by carrying gunpowder, but after the meeting with James they understand the position. It is perhaps not spelt out in so many words, but the intention is clear: bring back ordnance or there may be questions asked about what other cargo you have.

He spends many whole days at the manufactory in Edinburgh Castle. He is ordering bigger and better guns to be made.

'Do you fear war?' I ask him.

'Fear?'

I have used the wrong word.

'Are you concerned about possible aggression of King Henry, or some others?'

'A king can never relax for an instant.'

CHAPTER 10

The winter passes and the days begin to lengthen. James recovers his old energy and when he is not working exhausts himself and his men with long days hawking. He is often with me at Falkland, where the deer parks are good and the boar which my father sent are thriving and provide good sport.

Happy news comes from France of the marriage of my sister Louise. She writes that by the grace of God she has a good husband. She would like to come to Scotland and enquiries are being made about an easy route. I suppose she means through England. I recall how seasick she was and can understand that she should not wish to suffer that again. I tuck the letter into the bodice of my gown to reread later and go and find James to ask if he will approach King Henry to ask for a permit for Louise to travel through England.

He listens and then shakes his head. He will not ask his uncle for anything.

MY BABY is born in Stirling on the 24th of April.

As I lie exhausted I hear the cannon booming out over the town and musicians striking up in the great hall on the far side of the courtyard. David Lyndsay sends word that he has ready a poem of welcome for the new prince. Everyone is rejoicing.

I hold my son in my arms and smile contentedly at James as he stands by the bed. 'Two sons in the nursery,' I say. 'And more to come.'

The child thrives. He is baptised three days after his birth and I am told he wails lustily throughout the ceremony, a sure sign that the original sin of mankind has been driven out of him. He is named Robert for the earlier kings and most of all for the greatest of them all, my husband's ancestor, King Robert the First.

James's spirits are high. The birth of another healthy son has blown away the last of his fears. He throws himself once more into the planning for the decoration of the new palace, taking shape within sight of my window here. We both spend happy hours on the designs of the new tapestries. These are to be made here and not purchased from abroad. He authorises the import of more timber, for keels have been laid for two more warships, and I am to have the naming of them.

I rise from my bed quickly, before the week is out. I cannot abide the habit among some courts of requiring the women to lie in bed for a full month after the birth. It was not my mother's habit and it is not mine. James teases me that I have the sturdy body of a peasant woman and I take it for the compliment it is.

He has a map of Scotland spread out on the table in front of him and traces the route we will take on the journey he has planned for us. 'See here, we travel along the coast to Aberdeen, where they are preparing a formal entry for you. That is an easy journey, well-trod. Then we will come back through Huntly's lands of Braemar and then south again, for by that time the mountain passes will be clear of snow.

And then, when the weather is warm, we will travel to the west, to the islands.'

An usher enters. 'Your Grace, there is a messenger here, come from St Andrews.'

'Show him in.'

But as soon as the man enters, muddy from the road, I feel a chill, for his expression is one of despair. He drops to his knees before the king. He gasps out his message.

'Your Grace, the Prince James is ill. They ask that you come.'

James is on his feet. He seizes the messenger by the throat and I leap forward to grab his arm and pull him off. The messenger sinks back to his knees.

'How ill?' I ask.

But the eyes he raises to me are despairing. 'Very ill.'

'He was ill before,' says James. The messenger bows his head. He is near weeping, with exhaustion or sorrow or both.

I nod in dismissal and take James's hand to pull him into his privy chamber, but he almost elbows me aside.

'I will go to him,' he says.

'We will both go.'

'I will travel faster by myself.'

Word has already been sent to the stables, I do not know by whom, and a horse is ready for James. I stand with my women in the courtyard and watch him gallop away, two squires urging on their horses to keep up with him. I run up the steps to the battlements and watch him as he splashes through the river and across the plain until he is out of sight.

In the nursery the wet nurse has Robert at her breast. She has been carefully chosen. She is the daughter of a tradesman in Doune, one of my own tenants, for I have a small castle there. The family is known to produce healthy children. She has the light hair and freckles of many of the Scots. It is said they come from the Northmen who invaded centuries ago.

There is a low fire burning in the grate, for although it is almost May the winds still carry the chill of snow from the north. I dismiss my women and sit down with her and watch as the child greedily sucks the nipple.

'How old is your own child?' I ask.

'One month, Your Grace.'

'A boy?'

'A boy, praise be to God.'

'Who is feeding your baby?'

'He is being fed on goat's milk.' She giggles. 'I hope he will not grow up with horns.'

I resist the impulse to cross myself. The girl means no harm but it takes all of my strength to stay calm. I can feel the hysteria begin to rise in me.

When the boy has had his fill I take him in my arms. The cradle rocker comes to collect him to settle him for the night. I hand him over reluctantly.

I make my way to the chapel, where only a few days before the choir had sung at his christening in praise of God and thanksgiving for the gift of another prince. A year ago the same choir sang to celebrate the birth of my little boy James. I can sense my women hovering but none approaches me, or speaks. What can they say?

I kneel at the foot of the statue of Our Lady and pray harder than I have ever prayed in my life. I pray to St Andrew. I pray to St Clare, I pray to my dead husband Louis, I pray to my little son Louis, both in heaven, praying to them to intervene with God to save the life of my boy.

A noise brings me back to consciousness of the room. I become aware of movement behind me. There is a soft wailing noise.

I rise stiffly to my feet and turn to where the women are standing just inside the door of the chapel. In the flickering candlelight I see their pale faces, above their dark clothes, disembodied, their eyes wide. I look round. No one speaks.

'Has word come from the king? Another messenger?'

Still no one answers me. Then I see, at the far end of the antechapel, little Robert's wet nurse, crouched against the wall, her arms crossed over her breast. She is rocking herself backwards and forwards. It is she who is wailing.

As I approach the door the ladies step back and let me through and line up behind me, as if this were an ordinary day and we were going to join the court in the great hall. It is dark outside. I cross the courtyard to the palace. I walk upstairs to the nursery. I do not run. It is not fitting that a queen should run.

The priest is crouched over the cradle making the sign of the cross on the baby's eyes and mouth and chest. His tears drop onto the baby's face.

I look down at the body of my baby, my little baby Robert, named for the old heroic kings of

Scotland, so brave in war, so wise in governing and he is as dead as they are.

I DREAM I am carrying inside me a dead baby and I cannot expel it. When I wake the burden is still there, cold in the pit of my belly. I know from the taste in my mouth they have given me medicines to make me sleep and I am angry with them. How can I sleep when my babies are in danger?

I feel a sharp pain and open my eyes and see the black sucking leeches on my arm and the hand of the physician as he peels them off. I watch the drop of blood they leave slide down my arm. I am inside a bubble and they are all looking at me from the other side. None meets my eye. How can they? One of them murdered my babies.

They lie side by side in their coffins and slide together into the dark in the chapel of the Holy Rood. So they tell me afterwards. The mass soars to the rafters but the babies do not hear it. Nor do I, for I am in the grave with them.

When James returned from St Andrews that dreadful day he held out his arms to me, but it was not to offer an embrace, but to plead for help. How can I comfort him, when I have no comfort myself?

I am myself again. I write to my mother but her reply brings me no ease.

She is offended because she heard the news from others and not from me. She does not understand. I write to her the details. James, when he returned from St Andrews, was too incoherent to tell me much, but I made private enquiries. The baby prince was seen to choke and vomit and had a seizure. And then there were more seizures and then he was dead. On the same day my little baby Robert was found dead in his cot by his nurse.

I try to tell my mother this, and tell her I believe they have died by human agency, but she makes light of it. She writes that it is most likely Prince James died of overfeeding and that it is common for week-old babies like Robert to die. Death comes as easily to princes as to paupers. You are young. You will make more babies. No, she does not understand.

For there to be more babies there must be hope. And all hope has gone. I can see that in my husband's eyes.

My grandmother writes that it is the will of God.

I TRY TO PERSUADE James to hold an investigation.

'There is no point.'

'Poison. It can only have been poison.'

He murmurs something I do not catch. He repeats it. 'Finnart.'

'Finnart is dead.'

'He has taken both my arms, as he said he would. Next he will take my head.'

I write to my mother that my husband is bearing up well in his sorrow, that he is busy with affairs of state, that the court is preparing to go travelling and that the summer weather has come.

Only the last is true. James has withdrawn into himself. He means it when he refuses to investigate the deaths of the babies and when I say that even the dead Finnart must have had some human agency, he grows angry and turns his back on me.

203

I pour out my sorrow to my chaplain.

'Surely, surely,' I plead. 'Surely it is right that we find out who did this to my little ones, my harmless little children. Can you not ask the king's chaplain to persuade the king? Explain that the princes will not rest easy in their grave until they are avenged?'

He looks at me with eyes that are moist with the weakness of old age and not with sorrow. 'God will avenge,' he says. I want to write to Maître Guillet to ask him to return. He would be more understanding. But I cannot do it.

THE COURT GIVES the appearance of returning to normal. As we dine in the great hall I look round the boards. There are the king's gentlemen. There is Lord Fleming, married to James's bastard half-sister. There is Lord Seton, who grew up with him and loves him. There is Lord Somerville, known to be heavily in debt because he must make a show as great as any wealthy magnate. There is Oliver Sinclair, boasting about his new falcons to George Gordon of Huntly, who looks disdainful. There is Arran, whispering into the ear of Sir Ralph Sadler, a much subdued Sir Ralph, newly returned from England. Arran is smirking. I wonder who will drift to his side and seek to influence him. With the princes gone he is once more the heir to the throne.

'They fear for themselves,' David Lyndsay tells me. 'He turned on Finnart for no reason that anyone can understand. They ask, who will be next?'

There are my ladies. There are the friends I brought from France, fewer now for some have married and some have returned home and been replaced by Scotswomen. These are the wives, sisters and daughters of the great lords and chosen for expediency, for my favours must be as evenly balanced as the gifts of land and offices distributed by the king. What do they talk about when I am not there to hear? Do they talk about how they will rid the country of the French intruder and then the king can marry one of them? There is the king's daughter Jane Stewart, ten years old, just on the cusp of change, with the body of a child and the wiles of a woman. The king has an affection for her but I do not know her mother, who has never come to court. But does the child, placidly regarding me with the same black eyes that all the Stewart bastards have, report what happens in my private quarters?

There are all the court, the shifting crowd of lords and gentlemen, lairds and clerks, young men making their way, old men reminiscing about times past, all of them constantly seeking promotion and favours, grants and positions. Any man who can find a clean doublet and hose can join the throng around the king. Who knows what any of them might do for money or lands, if these were offered by some powerful lord or foreign sovereign who wishes us ill?

Who can I trust? I fold my grief up and offer it to God.

SIR RALPH SADLER has asked for an audience with James. James invites him to the privy chamber but when Sir Ralph enters he has to hide his surprise at finding not only several members of James's council but myself. Is this a formal audience or is it not? Is it an informal friendly meeting or is it not?

James greets him heartily.

The English ambassador has aged visibly in the short time I have known him. The death of Thomas Cromwell hit him hard, but he has recovered his own position and if the stories that come from the English court are correct, perhaps he is happier to be serving his king at a distance.

We know what he wants. There have been growing anxieties about an imminent war between France and Spain. Henry and James will each have to choose which side to support. François is tempting Henry with negotiations for a marriage between his younger son and Henry's daughter Mary. If he can but persuade Henry to support him, or to stay neutral, then he can throw everything he has into a war with the Emperor Charles. But everyone knows that Henry's instincts are always to make war on France and a war with France means war with Scotland. Henry's decision would be easier if he knew that Scotland was not involved, if James chooses to support neither side.

Sir Ralph does not say this. Instead, he raises again the possibility of a meeting with King Henry, who has long had a desire to know his dearest nephew.

'We have talked of it often,' he reminds James.

'It would be a joy to me also. How can it be arranged?'

'His Majesty thought, since you cannot spare too much time from the government of your kingdom, that perhaps you could meet somewhere near? York, perhaps. His Majesty proposes to travel to his northern realm this year.'

James nods slowly. 'Well, well,' he says. 'All things are possible. I'll give it some thought.' And then he turns the conversation to talk of the wondrous stories coming from the New World and Sir Ralph finds himself discussing the merits and demerits of different ship designs, of which he knows little. A rather wild look comes into his eye and he shifts uncomfortably in his seat. He attempts to reintroduce the matter of a meeting with his sovereign.

James is amiability itself. 'I will consider seriously my uncle's proposals. In the meantime, I have a request. With the winter the seas become dangerous for our merchants. Trade must go on. I would deem it a favour if Henry would issue letters of safe passage for them and their goods through England.'

Sir Ralph is falling over himself to assure James that he is certain this will be willingly granted. He is as aware as are all of us that merchants smuggle illegal books into Scotland. Is this a hint that such would be less unacceptable in the future and might our merchants, coming through England, bring such literature as would be approved by King Henry? Sadler cannot be sure what is behind the request, but he must take it at face value. He is clearly relieved when James nods his dismissal.

I catch a glimpse of Sir Ralph's face as he is leaving. He is not smiling.

There is silence while the men assimilate what has been discussed. They wait for James to speak first.

'I wonder what would be the result of a meeting with my uncle.'

'It could do no harm,' says Maxwell.

'What does he want a meeting for?' asks Arran. There is an impatient stir around the room.

207

Maxwell answers him, slowly, as if speaking to a fool. 'He wants to know whether James will support France against Spain or stay neutral.'

'He knows I cannot stay neutral,' says James. 'There is the French treaty.'

No one looks at me. It would have been well for Scotland if James's father had stayed neutral. He died for loyalty to the French alliance. If I were not here would James choose neutrality? His instincts are for peace at any cost. I have a longing to tell him not to involve his country in war, but I am not here to advise. I dare not speak. War is not a matter for women.

'How do we know,' asks Huntly, 'that his journey north will not be at the head of an army?'

'You should meet him,' says Maxwell, and several round the table nod in agreement. 'It would be as well to find out how the land lies, what his thinking is. His talk of war with France may be bluster.'

Treasurer Kirkcaldy of Grange clears his throat. James nods to him. Kirkcaldy clasps his hands in front of him as if in prayer. 'It is known that Henry has borrowed extensively from the Lombardy merchants. It is not clear that he could afford a war.'

'Can we?' asks James. Kirkcaldy looks unhappy, but since this is his normal mien no one expects an answer from him.

'If he wanted to prove his manhood we are the nearest and the most vulnerable,' says Huntly.

'Are you saying I cannot guard the border?' growls Maxwell.

'All the more reason to meet him, preserve the peace if we can,' says Tom Bellenden.

'He could be planning kidnap,' this from Oliver Sinclair. 'That might be his intention.'

They argue on. Maxwell and some of the others are strongly in favour of a meeting, Sinclair and others against. James listens, his eyes hooded. Soon he rises to indicate the discussion is at an end.

'Tom,' he says to Bellenden. 'You follow up that request for the benefit of the merchants. Go to England if necessary and obtain such letters of passage.'

'Why is that so important?' I ask James as the gentlemen bow their way out.

'It's not,' he says softly. 'But there must be seen to be negotiations on something.'

After dinner James quits the hall early and signals to me to join him in his privy chamber. He dismisses the servants and pulls my chair up to the fireside beside his own.

'Did you note?' he asks. 'Henry chose the time to renew his request when the cardinal is abroad. He knows Beaton would not countenance such a meeting, not for one moment.'

'Would he be so displeased?'

'Of course he would. He fears Henry might persuade me round to his way of thinking about the Church. And more than that, he dislikes the possibility of friendship with England.'

'There is no chance of that?'

He does not answer me. I realise that while I know the views of many of his advisers, some of whom would favour closer ties with England, I do not, even yet, know what James himself feels. Is the protection of the Church important to him?

'Will you go to England?'

'My absence would leave Scotland without a king and without an heir. Who can say what might happen when I am over the border? Oliver is romancing when he talks of kidnap. What I fear more are the fools here who would prefer I do not return. Besides, I cannot see much purpose in a meeting. Henry and I have nothing to say to one another. I do not want to be drawn into a war. I cannot afford it. I will keep Scotland out of it. We will concentrate on protecting our borders. That is as much as we can do.'

THERE HAS BEEN a long-standing promise that James would take me, his French bride, to the north to show to the people there. I am no longer a bride but now we must fulfil that promise.

It is a large cavalcade that sets out from Falkland. This is not a court obviously in mourning, for neither James nor I have the heart to care about any outward show. What do the symbols matter when our hearts are breaking? But when we pause along the way, women approach me with posies of flowers and whisper their sorrow to me. When this happens James turns his head away.

The weather is warm and the rigs round the hamlets scattered over this fertile plain are already lush with growing oats and barley. In different circumstances this would be an enjoyable journey and we would be happy. On our right the sea stretches to the horizon and the fishing boats come in as close to shore as they dare and sail alongside us as we travel and then veer off as the wind takes them. James watches the boats as they plunge through the waves and I know he is longing to be on one of them, fleeing to the far horizon and leaving all his cares behind him.

His mood is brittle and the circle of courtiers riding around us is silent for the most part, cautious in what they say. Sometimes he appears almost gay, singing in his harsh off-key voice which in happier times would make us laugh, laughter in which he would join, but now the humour is muted.

We stop at intervals and hold assizes at which James personally presides.

'The king is generally merciful, is he not?' I ask George Seton one day after I have sat in on one such assize. 'Is it not so?'

He hesitates. 'Any man may buy his way out of trouble with a fine.'

'Is that good?'

'For those who can afford it.'

There are long conferences with the local magnates and he is always with the lawyers, for he indulges his habit of rewards and punishments by the confiscation and granting of lands.

Our royal entry into Aberdeen is painful. The burgesses have long been preparing for this and I can understand the disappointment if they had to cancel it, but the content is unfortunate. It was all designed as a celebration of the happier times when we had babies in the nursery and they have not had the wit to change it. There is a particularly striking tableau of a girl who represents the Virgin Mary with the angel bringing her the glad news of the baby to come, and then this is followed by displays honouring the king's descent from Robert the Bruce and there are all his ancestors, all the Jameses. I pretend more pleasure than I feel. I owe it to these people to see their welcome as a gesture of hope for the future.

We stay a week in Aberdeen. James and his advisers sit every day at government business. I visit the shrine at Monymusk and pay homage to the relics of the blessed St Columba. At the convent I am made welcome and walk in the cloisters with the Mother Superior. I remember my days at Pont-au-Masson, when Mother was remote and frightening to the little girls like me. Now I find this one is just a woman like myself, worrying about the stores in their granary and about the well-being of the nuns in her charge, as I worry about the women of my household.

Then the angelus rings, the nuns file into the choir, I kneel in the nave and the voices soar above me, not as musical or as tutored or disciplined as the voices of the choir of the chapel royal, but true in their sincerity to the words they sing, and I weep for the girl that I was. But the past is done with and each day I compose myself and return to my husband's side and the secular entertainment laid on by the anxious burgesses.

In the evenings the students and masters of the King's College entertain us and we sit through orations in Latin, some of which I can follow, and Greek, of which I have none. The king hides his boredom well. I try to catch his eye sometimes but he is gone in some daydream of his own.

Word comes that King Henry has made his progress north and is at York.

'Did you tell him you were not going to meet him?' I ask.

'I never said I would. Why should he assume that he only has to crook his little finger and I will come running? I am not a dog to be whistled for.'

'Will he not take offence?'

'Henry takes offence at his own shadow.'

He calls a clerk and dictates a letter. 'What do you think?' he asks me. 'A gift of falcons. Will that soothe him?' He dictates. He hopes that his uncle the King of England is not too unhappy to be so far from his usual hunting grounds and he hopes the falcons will compensate him.

Cardinal Beaton sends word from Paris that King François is delighted that there will not be a meeting between Henry and James. He promises aid should Scotland be threatened with war.

CHAPTER 11

It is a wet afternoon at Falkland and we are relaxing with music and cards. An usher comes to tell James there is a friar outside, one of the brothers from the Carthusian Priory at Perth. 'Tell him that we will hear petitions for alms tomorrow.'

'He brings an urgent message from the prior, Your Grace.'

James nods to have him shown in.

The monk bows low before James. 'Your Grace, I bring sad news. The gracious lady the Queen Dowager your mother is ill. She asks if you could come to her.'

'What ails her?'

The brother is vague, as if speaking of the bodily failure of a woman is anathema to him. She cannot move and is speaking in tongues.

James is impatient with this. He dismisses the monk.

'Will you go to her?' I ask.

'No. She is always ailing. She will have overeaten or taken too much wine. If I go to her it will be a waste of a journey and she will seek some new concession.'

He signals to Master Taburner to continue to play and picks up the cards again.

And then word comes that Queen Margaret has died. Whatever she may have wished to say to James, or he to her, has gone unsaid.

JAMES LEAVES at once for Perth with Oliver Sinclair. I offer to go with him, but he refuses. 'You will be of no help.'

All I can do is pray for her soul and this I do. I spend time with the wardrobe mistress ordering mourning gowns for all my women and servants and a suit of black is hastily prepared for Dingwall Pursuivant, the messenger appointed by David Lyndsay to carry the news to the King of England. She was his sister and all must be done with honour and grace. Lyndsay as Depute Lord Lyon has the task of organising the funeral and the obsequies which follow.

His grief, at least, is genuine. 'I will always remember her as the beautiful young queen she was,' he says, and he quotes:

'The blackbird sang Hail, rose of most delight
Hail of all flowers queen and sovereign
The lark, she sang Hail rose both red and
      white
Most pleasant flower of mighty colours twain
The nightingale sang Hail Nature's best
In beauty, nature and nobleness
In rich array renown and gentleness.

'That was written by a greater poet than I will ever be. I remember her as a girl newly come north, who grew into a beautiful young woman and a gracious queen. Those were happy days.'

As he speaks Sir David turns his head away. His voice is full of emotion. 'We have never been so happy since.

'I started as a groom in the royal service and then became an usher. I had a modest talent for organising entertainments, so much of it fell to me. I became an intimate of the family. As far as any subject can become intimate. And then it all fell apart. I was with her on the day the king came to say farewell. He was going into England to make war on her brother. Came word that the armies were about to engage. The Queen and I prayed together all night.'

He balances on the palm of his hand the roll on which he has written out the order of the funeral procession. 'To no purpose. The armies met at Flodden Field and the king died.' He tilts his hand and the paper slides off. He catches it deftly with his other hand. He is near to tears. 'And so it ends.'

Cardinal Beaton is still in France. He sends his condolences to the king.

'He does not return for the funeral?'

'There is no need. Gavin Dunbar of Glasgow can officiate. Beaton never liked her. He was always suspecting she conspired with Henry. He will not be sorry that she is gone.'

Queen Margaret is buried with the maximum ceremony as is fitting for the daughter, sister, wife and mother of kings, in Perth, in the Carthusian Priory where her husband was laid to rest and where her children are also buried. The whole nobility of Scotland are summoned to attend. Until I came many knew no other queen but Margaret, who has been there for longer than many of them have been alive. There is much genuine grief and when the choir of the chapel royal are singing the new mass specially written by the canon Master Carver, I am in tears and I hear the sobs of those around me.

After the funeral we are shown in to the prior's room to rest. This is evidently a rich priory, for here the wall hangings are finely woven and threaded with gold. The cross on the prior's prie dieu is beautifully wrought in silver. Queen Margaret must have been as generous to them as she could be.

The prior fusses around, bringing wine and pastries with his own hands.

'Your Grace,' he says. 'I would talk with you about the last wishes of that gracious lady.'

'Talk then.'

If the prior wishes for some more emotion from the king he is disappointed.

'As she was dying the Dowager Queen expressed her wish that you and her husband, the Earl of Angus, be reconciled. It grieved her that there should be enmity between you.'

'Then I can only regret her wish must go unfulfilled.'

'Good Christian men should be united in amity under the Lord Jesus.'

'We may be united when we are both sitting in heaven at the feet of the Lord Jesus, but I doubt that even then. Her Grace my mother was a fool if she thought I would ever forgive the man for what he did to me.'

The prior bows. 'It is what she hoped to say to you before she died.'

I marvel at his persistence. This man, who must be twice the age of James, would have lived through the events of James's childhood and youth and his rebellion against his step-father. But then I remember my grandmother and how, even knowing the events in the world, she could continue to be unworldly.

'Then we were both spared the ill-feeling that would have darkened her last hours. Is there anything else?'

'She did not make a will, but she hoped that you would pass her few possessions to her daughter by the earl, the Lady Margaret Douglas.'

'Angus's daughter has chosen to make her home in England. Let her father provide for her. No doubt she has little need of a few old clothes.'

The prior looks at me and opens his mouth as if seeking my support but I give a little shake of my head and he falls silent. He bows briefly and goes. He must see to his other guests. James sits glowering at the fire.

I have never met the daughter of Queen Margaret. We occasionally talked of her during those difficult visits I paid her in her dark, unlovely lodgings in Canongate. Queen Margaret spoke of the girl with impatience. All the faults of the Tudors, she used to say, and none of the virtues. She was brought up at the English court and is reputed to have a wayward streak in her, falling in and out of love. While still very young she formed a liaison with Sir Thomas Howard. This angered her uncle, King Henry and he imprisoned them both in the Tower of London. She is understood to be with the nuns of Syon now.

I was happy with the nuns at Pont-au-Mousson. I was a girl, untried in the ways of the world. Even yet

219

I sometimes have a quiet yearning for the life of the veil. From what I hear of the Lady Margaret such a life would not be for her, but that may be her doom. Now she has lost her mother and must grieve at a distance.

'The girl is not responsible for her parentage,' I say. 'She is your half-sister and there are the ties of blood which must soften your heart towards her. She is in a state to be pitied. It seems hard that the girl should not have something.'

'She is her father's brat. The gowns will do in your own wardrobe.'

My ladies-in-waiting are always looking for new gowns but though they will not be pleased to have Queen Margaret's clothing, there will be some that are useful. There will be enough material in them which can be remodelled in later fashions than the queen was wont to wear. I wish I could have had my own people undertake the task of packing. I have no reason to suppose Oliver Sinclair and his people are dishonest, but much that is valuable can disappear at the time of a death.

'Her plate and jewellery . . .' I begin.

'There was little of it. It belongs to me now.'

I let it be. I will think of something to soften his heart.

'What are the books?' I ask.

He picks up the books which the prior has given him. 'This is the Book of Prayers which she was given by her father when she left England to come to Scotland to marry my father.' He turns the pages and reads out *Pray for me, dear daughter and remember that you carry God's blessing and my own.'*

220

He picks up the other. 'This Book of Hours was my father's gift to her on the day of their marriage. I remember her reading from it every day.' He hands it to me. 'Here is a portrait of my father being presented to Christ and St Andrew. The saint standing behind him is St James, the patron saint of our house. See, he has the scallop shell of the pilgrim. She often studied this page. It was always my father's wish to make a pilgrimage to the saint's shrine at Compostela, but it was never possible.' He closes the book and continues to stare into the fire.

I return to Falkland, leaving James in Perth.

I write to him that I recall the Queen Dowager had some fine Bruxelles lace. Would he save it for me? It has occurred to me, but I do not say it, that when it is cleaned I could send it to the Lady Margaret. It would be a small memento of her mother and may comfort the girl. I have so much lace on my gowns that James will never notice I am not using it.

He lingers in Perth, finalising his mother's affairs, dealing with the lands and properties which are now his. I send a message to ask when he will be returning. His reply is angry. He will be with me when he promised. As for the matter of the lace, he has not forgotten. I can sense his impatience. I cannot explain that I write to him of lace when I ache to write that I am anxious for his health. I fear the melancholy will descend on him again, but hardly dare say so, thus the correspondence is of trivialities.

Falkland is dreary these days, for in this time of mourning we have laid aside all gaiety. The minstrels pluck sad tunes in time with the steady drip of the rain outside. The king's gentlemen have dispersed to their homes with the promise to return for Christmas.

My women grow snappy with boredom and lack of exercise. They grow careless. The talk turns to the king and the wonderment that he stays away so long. They quietly speculate whether this woman or that is consoling him in his grief for his mother. Once I catch the name of Erskine.

They know perfectly well I understand Scots and do not need to have their whispers translated for me. I smile and order the minstrels to strike up a dance, the faster the better so that the women become breathless and the chatter stops. It stops for a while and it stops in my presence, but I know it continues when I am not there to hear.

The distance between Perth and Lochleven is not great. At night I lie awake and devils torment me with the thought of James in the arms of his mistress while her complacent cuckolded husband looks elsewhere and her clever son does his lessons in the next room. I should confess these dark thoughts. I could have talked of these matters to Maître Guillet if he were here, but not to the old priest who is now my confessor.

Some of the talk must have reached James in Perth, for he writes to tell me that the people who say he does not wish to leave there have lied to me and I am not to believe them. I reply at once promising not to listen to the gossips but to trust him. But still the talk continues.

I receive a letter from my mother which puts me in a rage. In it she says she has heard rumours that all is not well between my husband and myself and asks if I am being badly treated. I pace up and down my room in anger when I read this. Who has been carrying these tales? How dare they? How dare anyone comment on how I am treated when they are not here to see? She writes that my father is so distressed he plans to come to Scotland to see for himself. What does he think he will do? I burn with shame and anger to think that I, Mary, the Queen, should be so gossiped about.

Hastily I write back that what they have heard is not true. To make certain they understand I ask Madam Sancie to travel to France to reassure them in person that all is well here.

'Tell them,' I say, 'that we are only low because the last year has been one of sorrow, but our hearts are mending.'

JAMES RETURNS, the work at Perth done. Nothing is said about the delay.

Soon we move to Stirling for Christmas. The halls are still hung with black and the celebrations are subdued. I am ill with coughing and pains in my chest from the damp weather and spend much of my time in bed.

His mother's gowns are given to the wardrobe to do with what they will. The lace is cleaned and I send it with a kindly letter to the Lady Margaret Douglas at Syon Abbey, but she does not reply.

The cardinal comes for a short visit, for he cannot spare more time, his duties keeping him busy. He has with him a large household, for he never travels with a small one.

There is an ugly scene one wet afternoon. I cannot think what causes it, save that the mood of the cardinal is so opposite to the mood of James and the court. The cardinal has been away in France for the last few months and now he misreads the situation here. He interprets the dolour of the court as merely a formal show of grief for the Queen Dowager.

Thus has the cardinal been foremost in organising frolics fitting to the season. He has had his people create an Interlude on his favourite theme. It is as if, though he was not there, he has taken David Lyndsay's Interlude of two years ago and turned it on its head.

His principal character is a king, but what a king! He is enormously fat, as broad around as he is high. His breeches are bright green and his doublet white. There is a burst of laughter and applause, for these are the colours of the Tudor monarchs. He wears a gigantic gold crown topped with a peacock's feather. He wobbles across the room. A dwarf dressed as a priest comes running in behind him, pokes him with a pitchfork and runs off again. The king stumbles, the skilful stumble of the professional clown, and his crown falls off. He recovers it, places it with dignity on his head and glares round the hall.

Cardinal Beaton is laughing loudly at all this, but as he becomes aware that the little laughter around him is quickly stilled he quietens down. There are surreptitious glances towards James, who sits impassive.

The young people of the cardinal's household have been dressed as angels and demons and they successively torment the actor king and battle it out for the souls of the people, represented by various farmyard animals tended by simpering little milkmaids and boys yanking along model sheep mounted on wheels.

See, the cardinal seems to be saying, see the licence I give my people. And see, how we will prick the hubris of the English heretic king.

But the courtiers are not watching the masque. They are watching James. The Interlude ends in almost complete silence. It is with obvious relief that the actor king wobbles off.

The boys are lying around the hall still in their costumes, sweating and panting with the effort and drinking large gulps of ale.

'Thomas Maule,' says James to the page who happens to be near him. 'You did well. You were a bullock to the life.'

'The rear only, Your Grace. It is to be hoped that is not where my future lies, always at the hinder end.'

'It will be lad, if you persist in your marriage plans.'

The boy is instantly alert. 'Sire?'

He is a ward of the cardinal. He is a wealthy young man and his wardship is one of many lucrative such in Beaton's control. It is known that the cardinal has plans to marry one of his daughters to this boy as soon as he is of age, which I would judge from the fine down on the boy's chin will not be long. The girl is about the same age.

'You would do better not to marry a priest's get,' says the king, and his smile is pleasant and his voice gentle so that for a moment no one quite takes in

225

what he has said, then there is a sharp indrawing of breath and turning away of heads. Young Tom Maule looks stunned.

It seems only a little thing, a light conversation, a man giving advice to a young squire, but those round about us have heard. The cardinal has withdrawn to the closet but soon I see him return and later, over the heads of the dancers I see Arran speaking to him. There cannot be any doubt what he is saying.

WITH THE SPRING I lay off mourning and order bright gowns and a new riding habit of blue velvet. Each day's riding out with the hawks sees us returning exhausted and happy.

The threat from England appears to have lifted, for a letter comes in February from Henry saying he forgives James for his failure to come to York to meet him. He understands that James could not spare the time since he was concerned to subdue the far north of his realm, where he, Henry, has heard there is unrest. This is untrue of course. The north is perfectly peaceable.

James tosses the letter into the fire. 'There is more about the Church. The man is obsessed. He would have me break with Rome. What profit is there in that? He is a fool. He has despoiled the Church and for what? For some treasure which he has since dissipated. Whereas I can continue to receive homage and money from the Church if they wish to stay in existence. Which is the wiser policy?'

'It would not be possible anyway, would it?'

He looks at me slyly.

'What? To break with Rome?'

'Yes.'

'It would be easy, if I wanted to do it. When Tom Bellenden was in England he had a good look at the acts of parliament which Henry used. They were drawn up by Cromwell and would be worth copying. And if I call the Three Estates together two of them would support me. No, no. If I wished to destroy the Church I could. I choose not to.'

Whether those of his council who favour the new learning sense an ambivalence in the king and wish to take advantage of it I do not know, but the next council meeting is dominated by the question.

Lord Maxwell paces up and down the room. The man cannot be still for a moment. He has aged since those early days at Chateaudun when he stood proxy for James at our wedding. His hands, I notice as he thumps the table in his frustration to have his own way, are thick with blue veins.

'Ye canna stem the tide, James.'

'I hope it will carry us into a calm harbour,' says the king.

'Aye, well may it. But better to have the trouble visible where you can see it instead of creeping around under hedgerows and haystacks.'

The others in the council are quiet. Arran looks sideways at me then his glance darts away when he catches my eye.

Maxwell persists. 'Instead of all this trashy literature being brought in secretly by merchants, do you order a translation of the Bible into Scots and let the priests use it. Let the people have the word of God in their own tongue. That is all they want.'

227

'And have every man prey to the lies spread by those who try to interpret it for them?' asks Sinclair. 'Jamie, you cannot listen to this.'

Maxwell scowls at him. There has never been amity between these two and it was made worse recently when the rumour was spread that Maxwell trained his men on the borders by ordering sketches of parrots to be affixed to the targets for archery practice.

James sits at the head of the table looking from one to another as each speaks.

Tom Bellenden is also in favour of a Bible in Scots. He argues for a relaxation of the laws on heretical literature. If the Church suffers for it, it is because the Church is corrupt. 'When David Lyndsay performed that Interlude at Linlithgow he was tapping into the popular feeling. It didn't all come from his head.'

'Leave it in the hands of the cardinal,' says James.

From the expressions round the table, quickly hidden, I sense these men would not leave their second best cloak in the hands of the cardinal.

I HAVE PROBLEMS of my own to deal with, the continual problem of debt. A letter has come from the provost of the chapel of St Chapelle, whom I charged with saying perpetual masses for the soul of my dead husband Louis. These have now been said for several years and he indicates that while he is willing to continue without payment, he wonders whether my wishes have changed. He has also not received the timber he was promised from Chateaudun for repairs to the chapel.

I send more money immediately. M. du Feu has returned to France and it would appear that since then the management of my financial affairs has not been well attended to. I take it in hand myself. I discover that the extent of the calls of my very large household on my purse are greater than I thought. Income is not received as timeously as it could be. There are constant calls for alms, the latest I hold in my hand being from one of the convents of St. Clare, a sister house of Pont-au-Mousson that my mother has forwarded to me. I appear to be constantly in debt.

I make arrangements to check over the accounts personally once a month and tighten them up as every good housewife should. When James becomes aware that I am doing this he asks me to look at his own household accounts and this I do with pleasure.

Although I have to work hard and use every charm to overcome the resentment of his comptroller while I do this, it serves as a distraction from another anxiety. The winter has been cold and wet and in Stirling I never seem to be warm for a moment. Now it is spring and not much warmer. Cold winds blow over the plain and no matter what direction the wind comes from the palace is never free of it. I have an aching in my limbs and a general feeling of being unwell.

Worse than this, my courses have become irregular and may even have stopped. I dread I might be approaching the time when a woman ceases to be childbearing. Surely I have another ten years or more, but what if I am one of those women who are whispered about, who become unnaturally old before they reach the age of thirty? If this is happening then my usefulness to James is over. Some nights I wake up in panic at the thought. What will become of me when I can no long give him an heir? What will become of Scotland? The king is yet young and there are other women who will be eager to take my place. He despises his Uncle Henry and refuses to emulate him, but might he not be tempted by Henry's easy acquisition and discarding of wives?

I tell myself that I am useful to him in other ways. He takes me into his confidence, not always and not totally, but enough.

'James, have I been what you wanted me to be?'

'Hmmm?' He is lying on his back, satisfied. The curtains are drawn tight round the bed and I inhale the odour of his sex. I wish sometimes I could be more wanton. Perhaps this this would bring him to my bed more often. I have not confided in him my worries. I do not want to drive him into the arms of his mistress, if indeed she is still that. I can only be myself.

I move closer to him and he puts his arm round me.

'You remember,' I say. 'When you were negotiating to marry me and I kept refusing and would not be persuaded, you wrote and said you wanted a helpmeet, someone you could trust to help you govern your realm.'

There is silence for a moment. 'Oh yes,' he says. 'I remember.'

'Of course you remember.'

'Beaton said it would appeal to you.'

'Beaton?'

'He composed it. Was it really that that persuaded you?'

'Yes.' I whisper the word and can think of nothing else to say. The letter, which lies in my personal box of papers, has lost all of its value.

David Beaton. Beaton, who won a bishopric and then a cardinalship from the King of France for his skill in negotiating my marriage, busy, busy, charming David Beaton. David Beaton has clearly understood me more than I have ever understood him.

I continue to be uneasy about my health, until one morning I feel sick and suddenly realise that I have been very stupid. In my anxiety I had not recognised the obvious cause of my discomfort. I am pregnant again.

I tell James and he insists on an evening of celebration. He would have me sit and do nothing but the lively music has my feet tapping and I dance pavane after pavane. I bow to his anxiety and refrain from the gavotte which James dances with my ladies in turn, laughing and throwing them in the air. The gaiety is the more welcome for having been missing so long.

A LETTER FROM my mother tells me of the death of my little sister Louisa, in childbed, and the baby with her. I tell those of my ladies who knew her and then talk of it no more.

THIS PREGNANCY is different.

The four boys I carried high, but this baby sits low and causes me to feel clumsy and awkward. The women nod their heads and mutter that it must be a girl. Girls ride low, as if eager to be out into the world. I shush them. I would not want talk of girls to reach James's ears.

A letter comes from my son François. He is seven years old now. I seize it gladly and read the familiar opening *Je me recommende à la Royenne Madame*. He says I have not written to him and this makes him sad. I realise guiltily that I have not. My mother has often chided me in the past for my poor correspondence. My excuse can only be that I have much to do and much to worry me that I dare not put into writing.

François is growing obsessed with horses. The cornet his grandfather has given him is to be used when he goes hunting. He asks me to send him a Scottish horse big enough to carry him and his nurse, for he is supposed to carry her pillion behind him. He wishes I and my husband would visit him. His grandmother comes to see him in bed every night and gives him bread and cordial. The letter has been scribed for him but he has signed it himself. François d'Orléans. I feel the tears starting in my eyes. My son is growing up without me. I may never see him again.

The bustling women of the town barely glance at me as I am carried along on my comfortable, richly dressed litter through the streets. They are plainly dressed in grey and brown gowns, with only a kerchief round their shoulders, but they have babies on their hips and youngsters by their sides, solemn little girls and eager boys, and I envy them. Ordinary people can have babies or no, without a nation's expectations resting on them. They do not have to give up their babies to be cared for by others.

I suffer from palpitations of the heart and sleeplessness. My mother writes that she has consulted physicians who send their recommendations. I should take more care of my health to keep the ill humours at bay, I should live in healthy air beside the sea, avoid distress and remain serene and tranquil. I thank the physicians for their advice.

I feel an ache in my back and there is a spot of blood. I fear I am going to lose the baby. The physician is sent for. He advises rest and freedom from anxiety, just like his colleagues in France. It is easy to say. I spend the hot, bright days of July lying in a darkened room while my ladies take turns to sit with me, but I am alone with my thoughts.

The crisis passes and I am allowed out of bed but still I suffer from *ennui*. I have lost all my energy and my head aches. The goodwives offer herbs for both, but I am cautious now and take only medicines from women I trust. I have flutterings in my belly that are not the baby. I am full of foreboding. I, who have always been strong and healthy, now feel weak and weepy.

This may be the pregnancy that kills me.

I am haunted by memories of the babies who died, not just the two princes but my little Louis. I dream about my first husband. Queen Margaret always talked about the past and said reliving much of what had happened to her was a sign of death approaching.

I look round my chamber at the ladies with their heads bent over their sewing and wonder what they will do when I am dead and gone. Will my baby survive? Which of them would have the care of the child? Which can be trusted? Will James wed one of them when I am here no longer? Or will he look again to France?

I feel the hot tears coursing down my cheeks and bend over my Book of Hours in which I am reading the Virgin's song of thanksgiving but there is no comfort in it. This will not do. I pull myself together and send for the usher to bring quill and paper. I give instructions that I am to be left alone and go to my chamber.

I do not need to think too much of what I must write, for the words have been going round and round in my head these many days. I put down the heading.

A memoir for the case that I may die before I can carry out these matters.

I begin by begging my mother to carry out my wishes. I am confident she will do so. There are so many things I should have done. There are pilgrimages which should have been made but now there may be no time.

I start the list with the pilgrimages abroad.

From Scotland to the shrine of St James in Compostela to end in a High Mass.

Yes, that is an appropriate beginning. The saintly protector of James's house, a pilgrimage his father would have done if he had been able.

There will be taken an offering of wax equal to the weight of a child of four months. Another pilgrimage to St Nicholas of Lorraine, one to St Adrian in Flanders, all of these leaving from Scotland. Another to the three shrines of Our Lady near Chartres.

And then I think what pilgrimages could be done within Scotland. The most important is the shrine of St Ninian in the far south-west. James's father often went there. King Robert the First went there when he was already dying, so much was the saint revered.

Then I cannot forget St Adrian on May Island. Another to Peebles, to where James gave the gift of a piece of the True Cross.

And for myself, masses three times a week for my soul.

It is done. I lay the paper carefully aside. It will be found when I am dead.

DESPITE FRIENDLY WORDS from King Henry, James's intelligencers are reporting moves in England that augur ill for Scotland. Henry has asked his Archbishop of Canterbury, the heretic Cranmer, to research the old documents to find proof that he has suzerainty over Scotland. There is also talk of musters of men being moved northwards.

James is closeted with his advisers for hours and I no longer sit with them. War is not women's work. Women's work is making babies and now I am doing that again, I am not needed for anything else.

Sir Ralph Sadler returns, with more arguments why James should abandon France in the quarrel with Spain and join with England, but perversely, his master appears more eager to quarrel with Scotland than to make an ally of her. King Henry has renewed his complaint that James is harbouring Catholic enemies of England. They intend to raise a rebellion and James is encouraging them in this. Not so, replies James, they are merely men of conscience fleeing persecution. This does not appease Henry.

James suggests that a joint commission be set up. Henry agrees and our deputation is invited to London for this purpose. James sends Tom Bellenden, Lord Erskine and several others, men who can be depended on to be emollient with Henry, who will reassure him that they see his point of view and will do their best to persuade James towards it, but will be firm enough to keep reminding Henry that Scotland is not under his jurisdiction any more than are the Low Countries or any of the Italian states.

With the return of Cardinal Beaton from France the exchanges become harder, more bitter. It is as if his presence adds a new urgency. He has no doubts. The cardinal never has doubts. The enemy is Protestantism. The enemy is England.

In July the long-expected declaration of war between France and Spain is made and the time for hesitation is past. Henry supports Spain. He is now at war with France and war with France must mean war with Scotland.

Our spies report that he is strengthening his border defences. Norham, Etal and Berwick castles have been provided with fresh garrisons and Sir Robert Bowes, Henry's warden of the eastern marches, is supervising additional building work at them all. Henry has also sent the Earl of Rutland north, ostensibly to ensure that the peace along the border is kept.

'He has nothing to fear from me,' rages James. 'I am not such a fool as to waste siller on a useless invasion of England. What would be the purpose? Henry is seeing threats where none exist.'

He calls in Sir Ralph Sadler and rants at him. Sir Ralph merely stands there. He is not responsible for his master's actions.

A man is caught in the naval yard at Leith who has no business to be there. He was carrying a basket of fancy buttons carved from deer antler horn and going from ship to ship selling them. One of the captains became suspicious and had him arrested. Under questioning he admits to being a spy in the pay of the English. It was his task to assess the strength of our navy. Since James has a great deal of pride touching the navy, he thinks to let the man go and tell Henry that we can match his warships and more. He is overruled for once by the council and the man is executed.

'James, what is happening? Will there by war?'

'God knows,' he answers me. His face is drawn and I ache for him in his anxiety. I long to take some of the burden onto my own shoulders.

'We have managed to live peacefully with England these many years. There is a peace treaty. It is as if Henry wishes to force me into making war on him. It would give him an excuse to invade. He is getting old. Too old for war. They say his exchequer is empty. And he is now without a wife, so there is no hope of another son. Is this the last roar of a lion who sees life and energy slipping away from him?'

'What will you do?'

'What can I do? I can only try and keep the peace as long as possible. I've sent to Henry to propose a further joint commission to hold talks to extend the truce. I've suggested they meet at York. It will save time if our people do not have to travel as far as London.'

But nonetheless James sends out to all the magnates of Scotland to muster their men and be prepared to move at six hours' notice. The sheriffs of the west coast are ordered to bring men from the islands, fierce fighting men, to the mainland in case they are needed. All ordnance and transport is put on a standby basis.

The summer weather is fine and dry and I am finding my pregnancy easier. I wake one morning from a happy dream and though the details have fled, I have a conviction that if I make a pilgrimage then the threat of war with England will fade, that my baby will be born healthy. All our worries will disappear and we will be happy again.

The nearest shrine is Our Lady of Loretto at Musselburgh.

James, who is grey and weary, rouses himself to protest.

'You should not do it. You must do nothing to harm the baby.'

'Gentle walking will not harm the baby. This is a strong baby. Feel,' I take his hand and lay it on my belly. The baby kicks and he feels it and smiles.

'And we will make more after this one,' I whisper and brush his lips with mine. He holds me tight and sighs.

'Do what you must.'

I set off on foot accompanied by only a few of my ladies, but the king insists on Antoine following with mules and a litter in case I feel faint. He sends also several guards who walk at a discreet distance, some ahead and some behind. As we walk we pray and sing. The weather is fine and the sky clear. The verges along the road are bright with flowers, birdsfoot trefoil, lady's mantle, herb robert, shy violets, rampant peaflower and shading over them all, the white froth of meadowsweet.

238

There are other pilgrims on the road and despite my protests they are made to step aside while we pass. None seems to mind and when I look in their faces they are so absorbed in their own thoughts and hopes that perhaps they hardly see me.

As I walk I recall the other pilgrimages of my life. I remember the visit to the Isle of St Adrian with James. I try to recall our happy mood and the joy that followed. I cannot recreate that feeling, only remember that it was so. We were happy then, we will be happy again. Over and over the words tumble in my mind and I try to believe it. I close my mind to what came after.

I recall the pilgrimage I did in secret with Marie to St Andrews to pray for the king's return to health. It seems now to be in the distant past, but it was less than two years ago. The king did recover. I wish Marie were here now but a new pregnancy has taken her away from the court.

The shadows are growing long as we reach the shrine of Our Lady. Surely my prayers will be heard here, in this holy place built upon a stone brought from the sacred shrine of Loretto itself where St Mary the Virgin was born. I kneel and pray to her for the health of my baby and my husband and for the safety of the kingdom. As I rise to my feet I am overwhelmed with calmness and certainty. This baby is our pledge to the future. God will not desert us.

As I turn for home I am almost gay. I would have walked back to Edinburgh, so full of spirits am I, but my body is beginning to drag with fatigue and I am thankful to climb into the litter, where I sleep for most of the journey home.

AS THE SUMMER ends there is skirmishing on the Eastern Marches between small groups of Englishmen and our own borderers. This is not unusual and may not mean anything. The area is lawless, where the reivers operate, robbers and killers who care little whose cattle they steal and whose feuds are with Scots and English alike.

Then there comes a raid into Teviotdale which cannot be blamed on the reiving families because it is led by the captain of Wark Castle. Not much damage is done, but our people retaliate with a raid into England and burn the villages of Carham and Cornhill.

James sends a force under Huntly to Kelso on the River Tweed. At the same time he sends by fast messenger a letter to Henry. Surely these encounters arise because of the nature of the country, which is wild and little inhabited and the line of the border is uncertain. He assures Henry that he desires peace above all things and that any increase of men on our side of the River Tweed is purely for defensive purposes and to keep control of the lawless men who live in those parts.

Henry replies almost instantly that he wishes above all things for both nations to live in peace with one another and there will not be any further raids.

'I do not think we can trust that he means it,' says James. 'I have no wish to fight him. I wish he would govern his own realm and leave me to mine. We have no quarrel save of his making. If he goes to war in France the little pinpricks we can give him in his rear can hardly discommode him. He should see that.'

Within days a large force of Englishmen under Robert Bowes is reported to be marching into the

240

merselands. Worse, a rider comes to tell us that among the banners of the supporting lords has been seen that of the Earl of Angus, James's stepfather, his bitterest enemy. If the King of England wished to offer James the greatest possible provocation he could not have done better than this.

James calls his councillors together. They do not waste time trying to assure him that this is just another raiding party of little importance. This is war. This is invasion by an enemy and there is no way it can be argued to be otherwise.

No longer am I standing uselessly on the sidelines. I am the visible symbol of the alliance with France and that alliance must now stand firm against a mutual enemy. I am by James's side when he meets his council. I am there when he puts to the Three Estates the need for money to defend Scotland, when he meets the lords who will be leading their men into battle, for battles there must be.

Our men under the Earl of Huntly go out from Kelso and meet the English forces at Haddon Rig. There is great rejoicing in the court when word comes that he has overcome the enemy. Robert Bowes himself is captured along with several of his officers, including his brother and several hundred of his men. Any relief is muted when it is learned that Angus escaped back over the border.

'There will be worse to come,' says James. 'The dog has smelled blood. He will not rest till he has gnawed at my bones.'

The hostages are sent to various places to await payment of ransom. Sir Robert Bowes himself is sent to St Andrews as the guest of the cardinal and his brother

Richard, who has the reputation of being a very fine soldier, is sent further north, beyond hope of rescue, into the care of the Bishop of Moray. Others of the hostages are sent to Glasgow, to be held by the archbishop there.

Oliver Sinclair remonstrates with James.

'If the bishops have all the hostages, the English will think Scotland is ruled by bishops.'

'Then you have one of them.' And so Oliver Sinclair becomes the keeper of an English hostage, Sir John Withrington. In due course all these men will be ransomed and their hosts well compensated from the ransom money for the cost of keeping them.

Nonetheless the commissioners are still at York, talking to try and broker a new peace treaty. They send daily reports. The Bishop of Ross and Lord Erskine have instructions to sue for a perpetual peace, but the Duke of Norfolk, who is leading the English delegation, seeks nothing less than the end of the alliance between Scotland and France.

James sits with his head in his hands, the latest report lying crumpled on his desk.

'Henry demands a meeting with me. Demands, mark you well. No longer a request. And he demands hostages until such a meeting happens. What right has he? What right, I say?'

Andrew Learmont is sent to Greenwich with instructions to agree to a meeting between the two kings to take place in January. Now Henry insists that a perpetual peace treaty be signed before the kings meet. Henry also demands the return of the prisoners taken at Haddon Rig. James refuses. They will be released when both sides have disarmed.

'They talk and talk and all the time Norfolk is preparing to invade. My spies have learned of shipments of victuals from London coming north to supply Norfolk's army. They look for an excuse to invade.'

Henry sends his final demands. James must come to meet him, no ifs, no buts and notwithstanding my condition. Women, he alleges, are notoriously inaccurate when it comes to their dates.

This enrages me. 'That may be true of his wives. It is not true of me. I demand that Sir Ralph Sadler be sent for. Let him see my belly. Try to deny then I am near my time.'

But James will not allow this and I can only display my displeasure in private.

James's intelligencers report that an English fleet is sailing north with the intention of blockading our ports and even as we receive this report, another comes that the ships have been sighted. Our newly refurbished warship *Lion* is able to slip past the blockade and heads for France to advise King François of what is happening and to ask for aid. I no longer write to my mother. I cannot be confident that the letters will arrive and with an enemy on our border and spies throughout our land I cannot risk any missive falling into the wrong hands.

A Danish sea captain arrives at the palace with a message that help will be forthcoming from Denmark if England should invade Scotland. James receives this news with some emotion and rewards the captain well. It is a comfort to know that the nations of Europe are watching, but we are a small country on the edge of the continent and in reality how many will come to our aid?

We look for some respite. 'The fighting season is at an end,' says James. 'Thank God nothing much will happen now and perhaps by the spring Henry's aggression will have burnt itself out.'

But he is wrong. The Duke of Norfolk has left Berwick with his invading army. James's spies send the news and are not immediately believed, and then come messengers from the villages of Paxton and Hutton, and then from Stichills, Floors, Muirdean and other towns, as the army rampages and burns its way westwards.

'He is mad. The weather is against him.'

The River Tweed is in spate and some of Norfolk's men drown when a bridge is swept away. The land is flooded and already the first snows of winter are falling but he does not pause. He makes a large sweep along the banks of the Tweed, burning everything in his path. Town after town is destroyed. Many miles of land are laid waste and the people made homeless. They burn Kelso itself and its ancient abbey. There are few deaths among our people. They had warning of the duke's arrival and his progress, hindered by the rain, is slow enough to give them time to hide in the hills, but they have lost everything once more.

Now James orders full mobilisation and sends an army to stop Norfolk. All day and all night ordnance is being moved in vast cavalcades of ox carts towards the south. The people of Edinburgh stand silently in the streets watching as the dozens of cannon and cartloads of balls are moved out of the castle.

There are new weapons as yet untried in battle. Bringing up the rear is the biggest cannon of all, the one they have nicknamed Mons Meg. These armaments and the men marching with them are all that stand between us and the English forces.

BUT THE FIGHTING SEASON is over and Norfolk has to retreat to Berwick. His men are dying of the cold and sickness is sweeping through the ranks. Indeed, it is said that the duke himself has gone down with the flux from drinking dirty water. His men are starving. It was a cold wet autumn and the harvest was bad. The sodden land cannot provide fodder for his horses or bread for his men. Our spies report that he was too hasty in his preparations. He was ill-equipped and, believing his army would survive from the land they invaded, was under-provisioned.

But the damage has been done. The fragile peace which has lasted for several decades and which our commissioners have been struggling to extend, is over. Scotland and England are at war once more.

Someone brings to James a copy of a proclamation which Henry is circulating throughout Europe. In it he declares the cause of the war is James's failure to meet him at York over a year ago, but most of all because James refuses to recognise Henry's suzerainty over Scotland.

CHAPTER 12

The cardinal sweeps into Edinburgh at the head of a host of armed men. We hear his loud voice as he strides through the hall, through James's presence chamber and then he is with us in James's private quarters, exultant and glowing with purpose and energy.

'It is a holy war,' he says. 'We fight the infidel Henry.'

'My only purpose,' says James quietly. 'Is to protect Scotland.'

The cardinal hardly hears him. He strides up and down the room. He kicks at a log which has fallen from the fire. He opens the window, letting in a draught of cold air, leans out and lifts his hand in a blessing to the people in the courtyard below.

'At last. At last. I gave my undertaking to the Holy Father I would publish the Bull of Excommunication against him on English soil. Now, at last I will do it.'

He is determined. This man will never give up on something he wants.

'He won't rest till he has brought you down the same road as him, down the road to heresy. The Church will resist, whatever the cost. We will take the war into England itself.'

'I will not invade,' says James.

The cardinal is not listening.

'Once I have published the papal bull there all England is excommunicated. The people will not stand for it. They will rise and join us in defence of the Church. All they need is a leader with authority.'

'And is that leader yourself, Davie?'

At last the cardinal hears him. He stops pacing and puts his hand on his chest. 'Your servant, James. And Scotland's.'

James lets it go. Time enough when the crisis is past to subdue the cardinal's hubris.

'Has François committed himself?'

'He will.'

'He will have his hands full defending France against the Emperor Charles.'

'He will not desert Scotland.'

James shrugs at that. Time will tell.

The cardinal leaves then, his final word being a promise to raise a larger muster of men, even larger than his following camped now on the braes above the palace. He can do it. He has substantial Church lands under his control and he has the men and the money. We hear his voice and the babble of the excited courtiers in the hall and then the door closes and there is silence.

'I do not know,' says James, 'whether to be glad or sorry to have the support of the cardinal. The people will rally to defend Scotland. They always have. But will they defend the Church? They have given much over the years. Will they now give their lives?'

The cardinal himself leads his large force to the borders. I can imagine him on his favourite steed, White Bowis. In his golden armour and red robes he will be a pillar of fire riding across the plains. Although common sense tells me differently, I imagine him flaunting the Holy Cross, singing psalms and waving his crozier in the face of the enemy. If he cannot go to the Holy Land to fight a crusade, he needs must do it in England.

The response of the border lords is not one of amusement. They send a delegation to James. The borders will bear the brunt of the fighting, as they have always done. The people are tired of strife. They only want to live in peace. The men billeted on them must be fed, so precious sheep have to be slaughtered for the purpose, leaving no stock for the future. They are anxious to keep the English at bay but do not consider an army led by churchmen to be a worthwhile fighting force. They are not willing to provide any support.

'I cannot blame them for their unhappiness,' says James.

'But they have most to lose, surely?'

'Half of them are in English pay. They have been for years. They think I do not know. It matters little to them whether their king sits in Edinburgh or in London.'

'Cannot you force them? King François would not stand by while his men disobeyed him.'

'What with? Will gold persuade them? Am I as rich as François? Threats? I am not a tyrant like Henry. I rule with the consent of my lords, not against them. No, I will go myself and lead them in the defence of Scotland against England, otherwise all is lost.'

'No, James,' I say. He is gathering up the maps he was studying. I go up to him and sink to my knees.

'Don't, my dear,' he says and tries to prevent me.

'James, promise me you will not lead the army into battle.'

'I must.'

'You need not. You have good commanders. Please James, for the sake of the baby, please do not go to war.'

'It is not my choice.'

'Is this child to be left fatherless as you were?'

'Would you have me branded a coward?'

'Better that than dead.'

I bow my head so that I cannot see his anguished face.

'Please, James,' I whisper.

He raises me to my feet. 'I promise I will not lead my men onto English soil. That much I can swear. But if Scotland has to be defended against an English invasion, I cannot hide at the back.'

AFTER HE RIDES OUT at the head of his men I leave Edinburgh and return to Linlithgow.

I recall the stories my mother told me of my father, of his courage, of how only months before I was born he fought at the great Battle of Marignano, of how he was left for dead with twenty-one wounds but was rescued by his brother and rode afterwards in the great glory parade with King François. I replay this over and over in my head. When I was a child I heard only the stories of the courage, of the glory. I did not hear of the wounds that would not heal, of the half-lives lived by crippled survivors. I did not hear the anguish of the

250

women left fatherless and husbandless, or nursing broken men.

I am older now and wiser and no longer hear only the stories of the victorious.

I spend hours on my knees in my oratory praying for peace, praying that these men may resolve their differences. I pray, God help me, I pray that King Henry, old and sick, will die so that this nightmare may be over.

THE BOY COMES running into my quarters to warn me that riders have been sighted on the road from the south.

The men in the castle quietly take up their positions and the guards round the battlements stand ready. The drawbridge is pulled up. As the riders approach, the sentry at the top of the tower calls out that they bear the king's standard, and that there are only three of them.

It is James himself and soon he is by my side. Servants rush to remove his travel stained clothing, but he brushes them aside.

'Later, later.' I tell them to fill a bath in my bed chamber. This is no time for protocol. I will not sit quietly in my room while James makes himself presentable. I dismiss the servants and soon we are alone. He strips off his clothes and lowers himself into the water with the sigh of a tired man.

'I have ridden all night and all day.'

'What has happened?'

'Stalemate. Neither Scotsmen nor Englishmen will cross the border.'

'Not yet,' he adds.

'Is that it then? Is the war over?'

'Until the spring. And then it will all begin again. I do not think Henry will give up. Tomorrow I must go to Edinburgh and call a council meeting. We must plan for the next few months. But I wanted to see you to know that all is well with you.'

I bow my head at that and hope that he cannot see the tears in my eyes.

He heaves himself out of the bath and I towel him dry. He stands for a moment with his arms round me, awkwardly, for I am near my time and my belly is large. 'I have no heir, save this babe.'

'He has no father save you.'

'I was a king before I was a man. I must make sure that will not happen to this little one.' He rests his head for a moment on my shoulder, then all is brisk and busy again. He pulls on the clean clothes.

I am concerned to see that despite the bath and the clean clothes he has a beads of sweat on his brow. I wipe them away.

'Are you unwell?'

'An occasional shivering fit. It is nothing. Many of the soldiers have been ill but they recover quickly. Just a brief malaise. The living conditions are harsh.'

We dine privately. James still despairs of making King Henry see that his best interests will not be served by wasting men and arms on the border. The only beneficiary will be France, free to pursue her war against Spain without Henry's intervention.

'It goes deep, does it not? He seems to have a resentment against you.'

'All those years of trying to have a healthy bairn with first one wife and then another, and

252

knowing that if he died without an heir it might be I or my son who would rule England. My mother always believed that Henry could not forgive her for that. Do you think he rejoiced when our sons were born? Do you think he sorrowed when they died?'

'He has a son now.'

'The boy is sickly and there will be no more. But here we have another bairn coming. How much is this little one not yet born to blame for Henry's aggression?'

I send my chamber child away and James pulls the pallet bed alongside my own, for I am too uncomfortable for him to share my bed. I leave the bed curtains open and we lie in the dark, wakeful, and talk occasionally and doze. At this time of year the nights are long and dawn is a long time coming. But when the sky begins to lighten, James rises and kisses me farewell and then he is gone, without ceremony.

HE SENDS a messenger every day with word of where he is. Sometimes the messenger is Fergus MacLennan and I can question him more closely than the others. After consulting the council in Edinburgh James has travelled south to Lochmaben, Fergus says, and settled there with his men. He can travel either east or west, wherever there is a threat, although up until now all the trouble was on the East March, where England's defences are strongest. Lord Maxwell is patrolling the West March and the cardinal's army is at Haddington. His men will be held in reserve.

'Lochmaben's a lucky place,' says Fergus. 'It was the seat of the great King Robert and from there he rode out to defeat the English.' Then seeing my face, he hurries to say that King James will not be riding out to face the English. No indeed, for there are no English within ten miles.

'He had an ague before he left,' I say. 'Has he recovered?'

'Aye well,' says Fergus. 'A lot of the men have something of that. He looked fine to me.'

I send back messages of love and hope.

I AM TO GO north to Stirling, there to await the birth of the baby. This has been decided for me. Stirling is the most defensible of all James's castles and if there is trouble I and my baby will be safe there.

Leaving Linlithgow will take me further away from James and I do not want to go, but I am given no choice. Around me the palace is being stripped of furnishings, tapestries taken down, beds dismantled, clothes packed. Normally when this is being done it augurs a happy move, a progress to meet the people, for James to inspect a new deer park, for me to see how a garden I planted has thrived. Now it feels like running away.

I will not give the instructions to leave until it is necessary. All I can do is wait. The days drag. I sit with the women and listen to the drumming of the rain on the courtyard below us. The feast day of my birthday passes and there is no celebration. I am twenty-seven years old.

The child is heavy. Now, when I kneel at my prie dieu, I need the strong arms of my women to help me to my feet. I only have my French people around me now. The Scots have slipped away, the men to join the king, the women to return to their homes. If their men die in battle or are taken prisoner there are estates to be protected and young heirs to be supported in the hard times that will come. Many of them are too young to remember Flodden, indeed many were not born then, but the memory is seared deep and they grew up in the shadow of that great tragedy. They grimly prepare for another such. They care little what will happen to me.

I know enough now of Scotland to know that if my husband the king dies there will be civil war. So many of the lords claim a right to the throne and many would be willing to enforce this right with arms. My baby will not stand a chance.

NO MESSENGER has come today. I can sense the prickling unease throughout the palace. The messengers are brave men, loyal men, and while we are in this state of war with England they do not carry the king's badge but travel secretly and fast. Since James left for the south they have not missed a day.

But today no one has come.

Another night has passed. I wake with a sick feeling in my throat and cannot eat. I feel flutterings in my belly and wonder if the baby is coming, but it is not that. My women help me to dress. I take up my seat at the window from which I can see the road to the south.

A letter has reached me from Maître Guillet. He has fought his demons and come through the dark night of the soul. He hopes to be a better man. He feels evil forces gathering and he wants to be in the forefront of the defence of the Church. He asks leave to return.

Perhaps. Perhaps, after this is all over I will allow him to return.

Some of the villagers come running up to the palace eager to be the first to bring news that men, our men, bedraggled and weary, have been seen on the road heading west. They talked of fighting on the border, of losses, of defeat, of death, of our men taken prisoner.

'And we said to them, why are you here? Why are you not back there defending your king? But they just looked at us without an answer. They hadn't seen the king.'

The captain of the guard comes to me and says that it is time to travel north. We will not be safe here if the English have invaded.

Something inside me bursts free and I rage and shout. My women close all the doors between my privy chamber and the public parts of the building so that no one can hear me, but I want them to hear. I want them to know I am a woman of flesh and blood and I can feel as much as anyone. I scream at the old priest and ask him where is God. I scream at the women and ask them where are their brave men when the king needs them.

I stop screaming and start to sob and sob and when my gown is soaked with my tears my women ease it off me. They try to persuade me to drink a potion that will calm me down and make me go to bed, but I shake them off and swear at them in language which I learned from the gardener's boy at the convent in Pont-au-Masson.

But eventually I am exhausted and can do nothing except take up my station once again at the window, from where I can see the road to the south.

THERE HAS BEEN a confrontation between some English soldiers and Lord Maxwell's men. This much we understand from the garbled talk of the returning men. It is not clear on which side of the border it happened or even where exactly. The men say all the land round there looks the same. Round the River Solway is a land of quagmire and reeds. They did not know where they were.

More than one of them talks of a quarrel between Oliver Sinclair and Lord Maxwell, but what it was about they cannot say. Both men are now prisoners of the English.

'Lord Maxwell? Lord Maxwell has allowed himself to be taken prisoner?' I do not believe it.

Where is the king? None can tell me, until a bedraggled lad, an orphan boy who was a stable boy here and has returned to the only home he knows, innocently gossips with a kitchen skivvy. They are overheard and someone makes sure the news is passed to me, that it is believed the king has gone to Tantallon Castle.

Tantallon Castle is on the coast, east of Edinburgh. It was once the stronghold of the king's enemy Angus, but now it belongs to Oliver Sinclair, given him as a reward for his service to James.

I feel my heart sink when I hear this. Does he have a ship waiting there, ready to carry him away? Surely he will not desert his kingdom. Any danger is diminished. The English will be satisfied. They have their prisoners and the weather is now too bad for fighting. The Scots lords that are left can regroup ready for the spring. There is no cause for James or anyone else to flee. And he would not desert me and the child. Surely he would not.

I hear whispers. I hear whispers of a lady at Tantallon, a lady in the care of Oliver Sinclair, but not Oliver Sinclair's woman.

I do not ask about this woman. I do not want to know.

And then a runner comes to tell us that James is on his way here.

I summon all the palace to await his coming. It is not as great as the party he gathered together to welcome me to his kingdom, but I dress everyone in their best and all the men, even my Frenchmen, are in the king's livery. I order that banners be hung from the windows so that as he approaches he will know that we are welcoming back a king, a beloved king.

I am on the steps with my ladies in their brightest and finest clothes round me as he dismounts. I make my obeisance to him as best I can with my clumsy body and kiss his hand. He receives my homage with a smile and we make our slow progress through the people, who bow and murmur a welcome to him. A gardener's child comes forward with a posy of winter flowers, white and yellow, and if the petals are already beginning to drift onto the ground the spirit of the offering is clear. James takes it and pats the child on the head. There are tears in his eyes.

It is a time for protocol. He must go first to his own chamber to be stripped of his travelling clothes and bathe and then there is dinner in the great hall, in state, with all the people watching. I order my musicians to play as they have never played before and they put their hearts into it, but somehow even the lightest of the Scottish airs begins to sound like a lament.

There are loud voices at the door of the hall and I see some of the people being rudely bundled out by the guards. One of the guards comes to me. He speaks hesitantly. 'It was only some troublemakers, Your Grace. They are saying that it is ill done to be celebrating when men have died.'

'What is it?' asks James who has not heard this.

'It is nothing,' I say.

And then at last we can be alone.

He is ill. It is clear to me that he has not recovered from the sweating and shivering that affected him the last time he was here.

'They have not been looking after you.'

'Should I be comfortable while my men are not?'

He wraps the fur gown closer about himself and crouches beside the fire. I heat wine and add some warming spices. He sips it gratefully. 'I am glad to be at peace.'

'What happened, there on the border?'

'It was a pointless skirmish. Some of Maxwell's men met some of the English soldiers. By chance, I believe. Maxwell had no reason to seek a confrontation. There was fighting and Maxwell and others were captured. Oliver. Dear God, Oliver's been taken too. I sent him with my standard the day before. I thought that if I could not be there myself, then the men would rally to the standard. Perhaps Maxwell misunderstood. He took offence. They are saying his men refused to fight and he would not order them. I do not understand what happened.'

There is a pause and he speaks, almost to himself, 'I should have been there.'

I crouch on the stool beside him and hold his hand and the silence continues until James closes his eyes and sleeps.

The next day he is rested and has recovered most of his vigour. He is angry at the lords who deserted the army and fled into the arms of the English. He is angry with the cardinal. Where was he when he was needed?

'King François will send help,' I say, but he looks at me with a sad smile and shakes his head. He has lost faith in François. 'Just talk,' he says.

Now he is all action. He orders out men to search for deserters, men heading north and west to escape his vengeance. He sends word to Cardinal Beaton and others to meet him at Falkland, where they will plan for the future. I watch him signing these orders, his hand shaking as a fit of shivering takes him, and I watch the new heart and vitality that seems to seep into his men as they obey his orders. There is work to be done.

I want to go with him to Falkland but I am now too near my time to travel anywhere.

'As soon as the child is born go to Stirling as we arranged. I will join you there. Send me word and I will rejoice with you. Here is the future of Scotland.'

His horse is brought. His standard bearer is already mounted and waiting at the gates. James mounts, raises his hand to me in farewell and then he is gone, clattering down the hill at the head of his entourage and I watch until they turn north on the road to the ferry that will carry him towards Falkland Palace.

THE BIRTH PAINS are brief and the girl slips out easily as if in a hurry to be free of me. Many times in the past I have longed for a daughter, but Scotland needs a son. James will be disappointed. There will be more, I promise him in my mind, and there will be sons.

But no sooner has the messenger gone to tell the king of the birth of his daughter than another comes to tell me that the king is ill. The fever that was on him when he left here has worsened. The ride to Falkland was through early snowstorms and he rode without resting.

'I will go to him.'

But even as I try to rise from my bed, there are hands to restrain me. I struggle against them but they are strong and I am weak and I fall back on the pillow, exhausted and weeping.

Now all is quiet. It is mid-afternoon but it is already dark. The nurse is dozing on a pile of cushions by the fire. Trying to make as little noise as possible I move to the edge of the bed and sit up. I am dizzy for a moment but it soon passes. I slide down and stand on the floor and my bare feet scrabble around for my slippers. My head is clearer but already I can feel moisture oozing from between my legs. I am still bleeding after the birth.

I creep out of the bedroom. The door opens silently. In this palace all is well cared for, nothing creaks. In the presence chamber a couple of serving lads doze by the smoking ashes of a fire. The dog raises his head and then settles back down, but continues to watch me as I move towards the door.

I need clothes. My plan is to dress, take a horse from the stable and ride to be beside James. But even as I plan this I realise that of course all my clothes are in the great wardrobe. I have not needed to dress since I took to my bed for the birth and everything I was wearing has been taken away to be cleaned. I do not even know where to find a pair of stockings.

And then one of the boys wakes and gives an exclamation and my women come running and I am led back to bed and scolded like a child.

I am too weak to argue. I am helpless. I am a queen and nobody obeys me.

AROUND ME the great palace has fallen silent. There is no more music, or laughter, or the scurrying feet of clerks, or the shouts of the boys, or the clatter of hooves. I stand at the window overlooking the great court. The fountain is still, the pipes frozen. Already in my imagination I can see mould and moss growing where once the water flowed. An usher walks across the court. He is the youngest son of one of the northern lords. His father was not at the fighting. There is no reason for him to rush home. He disappears through the door into the kitchens and the court is once more empty and still.

When the news comes that James is dead it is no more than a ripple on the surface.

Fergus MacLennan is in the room before anyone notices. I am alerted by a gasp from one of my ladies. He stands before me, muddy, wet, his face blue with cold.

I do not need to ask.

'I have no lord now,' he says. He is sobbing.

'Will you stay to serve me?' I ask.

He shakes his head. 'I will go home.'

Now David Lyndsay is here and they are fussing round him, pulling off his boots and pressing a cup of warmed wine in his hand. He has grown old. He is weary and sad. He looks as if his race is nearly run. There are dark rings under his eyes and he has several days' growth of grey stubble on his chin.

'I was with him at the end,' he says.

'Did he suffer?'

'He was delirious. The illness,' he hesitates for the word, this man of words. 'The illness had taken a hold of his mind as well as his body.'

'What will happen now?'

'I have come to warn you. They have a document which they claim is the king's will.'

'Claim? Do you not believe them?'

'I cannot see how he was able to give instructions.'

'What does it say?'

'In it James appoints a Council of Regency.'

'But surely I will be regent. Surely that is the custom here?'

'It has been the custom in the past. Queen Margaret acted as regent for Jamie up till the time she remarried and lost it.'

'That is a mistake I will not make.'

But I can see clearly what they must all be thinking. A female regent for a girl child? It has never been known.

'Who is named in this alleged council?'

He lists the names, expressionless. 'Argyll, Huntly, Moray, the cardinal of course.'

'Of course. The Earl of Arran?'

'They do not want him. He is considered unstable.'

'Was he there? With the king?'

'No. He has gone to Hamilton, to his estates there.'

Perhaps he is already raising an army.

'What will happen now?'

'They will come and ask you what you want. Under the terms of your marriage settlement you can return to France. You would still keep the revenues granted you by the king. You would be wealthy and comfortable back in your own land.'

I am not wanted here.

'My daughter?'

'She would have to stay here. She is the queen now.'

Outside the window the snow is drifting down in great white flakes. I think of Chateaudun and the heat of the sun and the mid-day rains that settle the dust and cease as quickly and suddenly as they start, leaving only a mist hovering above the hot stones of the terrace.

I listen to the silence of the great cold palace round me. I hear again the silence of the convent. I sense the silence of the grave.

My ladies are huddling in the far corner of the chamber, out of earshot. I signal to them and they come forward eagerly. I tell them to give instructions to the steward. We will leave for Stirling as soon as it is light in the morning. They protest. The baby is too young to be moved. The weather is not suitable for travelling. But I insist. We will go to Stirling Castle, which can be defended against any siege. The men are to finish packing up. Anything not packed will have to be left.

David Lyndsay begins to tell me that there is no need for such speed. We are safe at Linlithgow for there will be no more aggression from the English now that they have such valuable prisoners. The Scottish lords will do nothing to harm me or the baby.

'You mean well, my old friend, and I thank you. But I will take my daughter to Stirling where she will be safe.'

Once more I have no husband. In the past the decisions were made for me and despite me. Now I will make my own decisions and none shall overrule me. My daughter depends on me and I will depend on no one.

I turn back to Sir David. 'I will not return to France. I will keep this realm safe for my daughter. And for God. This I swear. Scotland is my home now.'

SELECTED BIBLIOGRAPHY

Balcarres Papers, *The Foreign Correspondence of Marie de Lorraine, Queen of Scotland 1537-1548*, ed. Marguerite Wood, Publ. by the Scottish History Society

Cameron, Jamie, *James V, the Personal Rule 1528 – 1542* (Tuckwell Press, 1998)

Cowan, I.B. (ed.) *Blast and Counterblast, Contemporary Writings on the Scottish Reformation* (The Saltire Society, 1960)

Fraser, Antonia, *Mary Queen of Scots* (Orion paperback edition, 2009)

Friar, Stephen & Ferguson, John, *Basic Heraldry* (The Herbert Press, 1993)

Historic Scotland, *Stirling Castle, Official Guide* (2011)

Knox, John, *The History of the Reformation in Scotland* (The Banner of Truth Trust, 1982 edition)

Lamont, Stewart, *The Swordbearer: John Knox and the European Reformation* (Hodder & Stoughton, 1991)

Lamont-Brown, Raymond, *St Andrews, City by the Northern Sea* (Birlinn, 2006)

Lyndsay, Sir David, *Ane Satyre of the Thrie Estates* (Canongate Classics, 1989)

MacCulloch, Diarmaid, *Reformation 1490–1700* (Penguin, 2003)

Marshall, Rosalind K., *Mary of Guise* (Wm Collins Sons & Co. Ltd. 1977)

Mapstone, Sally & Wood, Juliette (eds.) *The Rose and the Thistle, Essays on the Culture of late Medieval and Renaissance Scotland* (Tuckwell Press, 1998)

Reid, Harry, *Reformation, The Dangerous Birth of the Modern World* (St Andrew Press, 2009)

Sanderson, Margaret H.B., *Cardinal of Scotland* (John Donald Publishers Ltd., 1986)

Thomas, Andrea, *Princelie Majestie: The Court of James V of Scotland* (Birlinn, 2005)

Wormald, Jenny, *Court, Kirk and Community, Scotland 1470 - 1625* (Edinburgh University Press 1981)

Yeoman, Peter, *Pilgrimage in Medieval Scotland* (Historic Scotland, 1999)